FOUR CORNERS VOICES

Stories | Poetry | Essays

Volume 2

FOUR CORNERS
VOICES
Stories · Poetry · Essays

Volume 2

Edited by:

Gail Binkly • Sarah Carr

Chuck Greaves

WRITERS

Contents

Essays

Introduction

Welcome to this second anthology of essays, poetry, and stories from over forty talented authors, brought to you by Four Corners Writers, a Colorado-based nonprofit whose mission is to identify, develop, and promote literary voices in the American Southwest.

As with its predecessor, *Four Corners Voices*—winner of the 2025 Colorado Book Award—these works were selected from an open competition that attracted over 180 submissions from a broad demographic spectrum of writers based in, or writing about, the canyon-filled and mountain-rimmed landscapes shared by Colorado, Utah, Arizona, New Mexico, and the Ute Mountain Ute and Navajo Tribal Nations. The result, as you're about to discover, is a delightful compendium of creative expression that will transport the reader to one of America's most iconic and breathtaking landscapes, viewed through the compound, kaleidoscopic lens of some of its most diverse and talented voices.

Four Corners Writers would like to thank the LOR Foundation and the Ballantine Family Fund for helping underwrite this effort. More importantly, we'd like to thank you, the reading public, for making our first anthology such a smashing success—did we mention that Colorado Book Award?—and for once again joining us on this transformative journey of discovery, enchantment, and adventure.

The 2025 Editors:
Gail Binkly (Essays)
Sarah Carr (Poetry)
Chuck Greaves (Stories)

Vaquera

Kim Henderson

The summer Tabby is nineteen and tired of being the girl whose college instructors forget her name, she spots an ad for mascot tryouts in the community college newspaper and finds herself at the audition doing cartwheels and strutting like Yosemite Sam in front of a scowling cheerleading coach and her squad. She gets the job, savors a rare instance of being handpicked, and prepares to become Valo the Vaquero—actually, one of three Valos who rotate, costumed in chaps and a giant cowboy hat, thick handlebar mustache, bushy unibrow, and jutting cleft chin.

Her father finds out and drags her to the shed to sort through a box of spurs from his bull riding days.

"I don't need those," she says, batting at the swirling dust. "My costume came with spurs."

"But mine will be authentic—I wore them to ride Maverick Mudslinger when I was your age. So, when can I come watch you?"

She rolls her eyes. "There's nothing to *see*." She hangs out the shed door to suck in slightly less stifling air and watches a dust devil whip through the neighbor's field of creosote bush. "I'll just be entertaining little kids. You don't want to watch me babysit."

He pulls a worn spur out of the box, flakes of ancient manure floating onto his shirt, and grins. "I want to see my little spitfire wowing the crowd."

On the first day of practice, the cheerleading coach paces in front of the three Vaqueros and says, "The most important thing is to never break character." She pauses in front of Tabby. "When you aren't performing with the cheerleaders or setting up for a contest or entertaining crying babies, you don't just sit on your chaps. You strut through the stands, or practice with your lasso, or rubberneck pretty ladies. You think cheerleaders get tired? You don't know tired until you are the Vaquero."

Tabby discovers, slipping into canvas pants and buttery chaps, that maybe she has always been a vaquero and didn't know it— maybe she just needed a mask. She revels in the humid sweat trapped in her big plastic man-face, accepting the inevitable acne and sore shoulders as she lassoes child after child to reel them in for hugs and photos. Between innings, she sprints onto the field to host contests where women race to rope their partners and children hop to the finish line in gunny sacks. Someone tells her she is the liveliest mascot they've ever seen, and she tucks her thumbs into her belt loops and kicks the ground with a pointed boot.

Her father is relentless: he wants to see her *perform*. Why won't she let him see her *perform*?

"Fine," she says, but her chest tightens and her shoulders draw up at the thought of it. She sends her parents to a game on her night off, and while her plan is to hide in the library and meet them outside afterward, she can't resist sneaking in to watch them watching her.

She sits near third base and spots them behind home plate. Her father's teeth flash as Valo struts nearby—tonight a muscled, acrobatic girl named Holly. She doesn't interact with spectators as much as Tabby, but she bounds through roundoffs and handsprings in the seventh inning stretch that Tabby doesn't have the strength, balance, or stamina to stick. Tabby watches her parents' faces closely for surprise, doubt, realization. But they merely beam, and as ballplayers take the field, her father catches the Vaquero's attention and spins an imaginary rope above his head.

She lets him reel her in, but after posing for a snapshot she moves on, though he continues to wave and holler. It reminds Tabby of school plays when she'd see his big, expectant smile in the audience, his sparkling eyes waiting for recognition. No matter how well she'd done in rehearsals, she'd inevitably break character to give him a smile or a wave. This Valo, though, gives no nod or knowing signal, and instead ignores the fanatic in the stands.

When, after the fifth inning, the Vaquero doesn't launch a t-shirt his way, her father struts down the steps and snatches one from the bag at her side, smiling red-faced at the crowd. Holly storms to security with a confidence Tabby could never muster. It is then that Tabby sees him realize, as he buries his teeth behind his lips, grabs her mother by the arm, and storms out.

Tabby tiptoes home and waits for morning, which finds him splayed beneath his truck, banging on the starter with a socket and cussing over the wail of a country song. She twists her early shadow and clears her throat until he scoots out and asks what she wants. When she opens her mouth to spill the truth, to confess her fear of shifting from steely-eyed vaquero into tail-tucking burro under his ever-watchful gaze, their eyes meet and what comes out instead is, "Why do you always have to embarrass me?" and once it is in the air she realizes this is also true, and that no matter how things might have gone at the game, the night would have ended the same.

He says nothing and glides back under the truck, where he will pretty much remain for the rest of summer. In less than a year, he will be dead, his head smashed at work by a truck a lot like this one, and while their relationship will have been mostly patched up, for a long time this is the memory that will wake her: him flashing that big, bright grin and waving, waving, waving at a girl he adored who neither could admit wasn't her.

Kim Henderson is the author of the prize-winning fiction chapbook, The Kind of Girl *(Rose Metal Press). Her stories have appeared in* The Kenyon Review, The Missouri Review, Tin House Online, Story, *and elsewhere. She teaches writing at San Juan College in Farmington.* "Vaquera" *originally appeared in* Flash Fiction Online.

Recipe for the Wild

David Feela

In the middle of August
on Kennebec Pass
a forest service sign warns me

bears are in the area.
I plant my tent, stake it
to the earth, then hike a circle

around my camping spot.
Bending to penetrate
the thick undergrowth,

I smile as two red spheres
stare back at me:
berries are in the area too,

raspberries ripe as summer.
Dozens more appear
where the two had been,

then hundreds, perhaps thousands
and the two clumsy cups of my
bare hands can't contain them.

Birds in the trees chide me,
taking only a few at a time
but I fill one hand,

spill those berries into my mouth,
lick the juice from that hand
and fill the other.

I am ravenous for this serum
of wildness to heal my blood.
Before frost comes to this place,

before snow narrows the path
to impassable, I want to grow fat
on raspberries, to stumble back

to my tent and sleep, maybe not stir
until the tiny white flower
of morning unfolds.

David Feela has published three books of poetry. His earlier essay collection, How Delicate These Arches *(Raven's Eye Press, 2011), was a finalist for the Colorado Book Award.* Feelasophy: Selected Essays *is his second collection of essays. He lives in Cortez. Visit davidfeela.com to view his website. "Recipe for the Wild" was previously published in* Bristlecone Magazine.

Solving Everett Ruess

C h u c k   G r e a v e s

On November 12, 1934, a peripatetic young artist named Everett Ruess loaded up his pack burros, said goodbye to the friends he'd made in the remote Mormon settlement of Escalante, Utah, and resumed a journey of exploration, both cartographic and spiritual, that had come to define his young life. His intention, as expressed in letters he'd posted to his family in California, was to travel south—either across the Colorado River at Lee's Ferry and back onto the Navajo reservation from which he'd come, or else into the maze of side canyons marking the Escalante River's confluence with the Colorado, and thence eastward, crossing the latter somewhere above its junction with the San Juan River gorge.

He was never heard from again.

That same day, less than 50 miles to the east, a 36-year-old Texas drifter named James Clinton Palmer was building a crude dugout shelter in which to spend the coming winter in the company of a ragged, visibly-pregnant 14-year-old whom he called Johnny Rae.

The disquieting couple had been hired by Monument Valley trading-post owner Harry Goulding to tend a flock of sheep that had, just a few months earlier, been ordered north of the San Juan River by federal authorities when their home range became part of the Navajo reservation in 1933. Not surprisingly, this sudden influx of over 1,500 hungry sheep precipitated a series of escalating conflicts with the Mormon cattlemen on whose traditional stock range the Goulding sheep now foraged.

What Goulding did not know was that the man he'd hired was a violent psychopath recently released from the federal penitentiary in Leavenworth, Kansas. Or that Palmer had, only a few months earlier, kidnapped his child bride—whose real name was Lucile "Lottie" Garrett—from Oklahoma after murdering and decapitating her father. Or that Palmer would soon be murdering again, in similarly-gruesome fashion.

The red rock country of southern Utah—with its canyons and mesas, its spires and gorges—is among the most beautiful and, paradoxically, among the least populous regions in America, and when Everett Ruess vanished into its rugged dreamscape in November of 1934, he passed into legend. No fewer than five books and two documentary films have celebrated the young man Wallace Stegner called an "atavistic wanderer of the wastelands," and about whom John Nichols wrote, "it was his life that was his greatest work of art." His disappearance remains—along with those of Amelia Earhart and Joseph Force Crater—one of the enduring mysteries of the Twentieth Century.

Speculation over the fate of Everett Ruess has run rampant ever since his pack burros and a few personal effects were discovered in remote Davis Gulch—northwest of the Colorado River's confluence with the San Juan River—on March 3, 1935. Searchers soon discovered his trademark "NEMO 1934" graffito etched into the high-desert sandstone of a nearby Ancestral Puebloan ruin. Of the boy, however, there was no further sign.

Theories advanced to explain the Ruess mystery have ranged from the prosaic—he fell to his death, or he drowned—to the fantastic. Some say he was murdered, or took his own life. Some say he never died at all, but rather slipped onto the Navajo reservation, took a Native bride, and lived to old age in quiet anonymity. In April of 2009, *National Geographic* magazine entered the fray, reporting a Diné grandparent's supposed deathbed account of Everett Ruess's murder at the hands of three Ute Mountain Ute assailants. Initial DNA testing of skeletal remains raised hopes that the 75-year mystery had at last been solved. Those hopes were dashed, however, when further testing confirmed the purported Ruess remains to be of Diné ancestry.

There is, however, one solid clue to the fate of Everett Ruess, which came to public light in 1983 when Escalante river guide Ken Slight (the real-life inspiration for Seldom Seen Smith, of *The Monkey Wrench Gang* fame) discovered another NEMO etching in lower Grand Gulch, also north of the San Juan River, some 40 miles due east of the 1934 Davis Gulch discovery. According to Southwest author and historian Fred Blackburn, who personally took tracings of the two graffiti, they indicate a common hand.

If Ruess was, in fact, hiking eastward, exploring the cuts and canyons along the northern rim of the San Juan River gorge, perhaps working his way toward the bridge crossing at Mexican Hat, then he soon would have entered John's Canyon, less than ten miles due east of Grand Gulch, probably in late November or early December of 1934.

And there he would almost certainly have encountered Clint Palmer.

By Thanksgiving of 1934, complications in young Lucile's pregnancy required that she return to Goulding's Trading Post in Monument Valley, where she remained until December 11 and then was moved to Monticello, Utah, giving birth on December 31 to a baby boy who would die seven days later. By mid-January, she and Palmer were back in their John's Canyon dugout, and the long-simmering range war over the Goulding sheep would soon come to a boil.

On February 28, 1935, as Palmer once again drove the Goulding flock into John's Canyon for water, he encountered Blanding cattleman William E. Oliver, age 77, the former sheriff of San Juan County, Utah. Oliver was one of—and arguably the last of—the legendary frontier lawmen, thanks to his central role in Posey's War, America's "last Indian uprising." In that 1923 incident, Sheriff Oliver's horse had been shot out from under him during a daring escape attempt by a pair of Ute prisoners, in response to which Oliver held over 40 Ute men, women, and children hostage in a Blanding stockade in a tense, month-long armed standoff.

Bill Oliver was not, even in retirement, a man to be trifled with.

Inside John's Canyon, words were exchanged between Palmer and Oliver, and shots were fired, and the former sheriff fell dead beside his horse. After dragging Oliver's body to the river gorge, Palmer set off on horseback to find Norris "Jake" Shumway, Oliver's 25-year-old grandson, whom Palmer then shot and decapitated, eliminating his only potential witness.

The next day, Palmer and Lottie appeared in Monument Valley, where at gunpoint they relieved Harry Goulding of his car and 40 dollars in cash before lighting out for Texas. Unbeknownst to the fleeing outlaws, however, the decapitated skeleton of Lucile's father had since been discovered and placed on display at the Hopkins County courthouse in Sulphur Springs, and a Texas warrant was outstanding for Palmer's arrest. The pair was finally apprehended on March 5, 1935, and the resulting Greenville, Texas "skeleton murder" trial—featuring Lucile Garrett as its star witness—was a regional sensation.

According to this blood-soaked timeline, Clint Palmer—already psychotic, and heavily armed, and under growing pressure from all sides—was alone in Utah's John's Canyon from Thanksgiving of 1934 until mid-January of 1935. Did Everett Ruess, whom we now believe to have been but ten miles away, and heading in Palmer's direction, wander into Palmer's sheep camp? And if so, did he meet the same fate as had befallen Dillard Garrett, and soon would befall Oliver and Shumway?

On the same day—March 7, 1935—that the *San Juan Record* first reported the John's Canyon killings in a banner headline proclaiming DOUBLE MURDER SHOCKS COUNTY, it also reported, in the adjoining column on page one, the disappearance of a young, unnamed artist who had last been seen in November of 1934 near the Escalante River, where "[p]lanes were used to try and locate the artist's camp and succeeded in finding what they thought to be the pack burrow [sic] which he used. No camp or other sign of the lost man have yet been found."

Harry Goulding is today best known as the man who brought Hollywood to Monument Valley when, in 1937, he drove his battered truck to Los Angeles with a bedroll and a stack of photographs and managed to convince director John Ford to film *Stagecoach*—a planned Western epic starring a young stuntman named John Wayne—on a Navajo reservation reeling from a half-decade of drought and Depression.

Pioneer, promoter, and trading-post impresario, Goulding was a Western character writ large whose life has been chronicled in books like Samuel Moon's *Tall Sheep* (1992), and Richard E. Klinck's *Land of Room Enough and Time Enough* (1995), and in the March 2009 issue of *Vanity Fair* magazine (Bissinger, "Inventing Ford Country.") But there is one subject on which even the loquacious Harry Goulding would remain forever silent, right up until his death in 1981:

"Harry never defended himself to the people of Blanding, and forty years later he would not speak to me on the record about his part in the Jimmy Palmer affair. True to his western values, he believed that a man should be judged by his actions, not by his words, and that his life would have to speak for him. Ultimately, it seems that we must leave it where Harry wanted us to leave it." Moon, *Tall Sheep*, at 87.

In contrast to the gauzy glow of legend that has come to envelop Everett Ruess, the John's Canyon murders of Bill Oliver and Norris Shumway are but forgotten footnotes in the long and sometimes colorful history of San Juan County, Utah. In November of 1993, however, I stumbled upon a pair of human skulls while hiking in John's Canyon. That discovery would lead me to undertake years of painstaking research into the John's Canyon murders, their etiology, and their consequences—research that grew to encompass newspaper accounts, court and prison records, genealogical and oral histories, and (in the archives of a Salt Lake City museum) re-discovery of the "lost" 1935 grand jury testimony of Harry Goulding.

My novel *Hard Twisted*, based on the true story of Lottie Garrett's harrowing year in captivity, was published by Bloomsbury in November of 2012. It opened the door on a long-forgotten chapter in Western history. Did it also hold the key to the seemingly insoluble mystery of Everett Ruess?

Chuck Greaves/C. Joseph Greaves is the author of seven novels including Hard Twisted *(Bloomsbury), which the* Los Angeles Times *hailed as "a gritty, gripping read, and one that begs to be put on film." You can visit him at www.chuckgreaves.com.*

When He Speaks in *Diné Bizaad*

Z o e y   Y a z z i e   /   (y) a z

—i can still see the dash
     of your lightning bolt smile
       —and the hot splash of
        Ray-Ban aviator blues
        with blood sausage and
         mudstone monologue
          dripp—
             i
               n
                 g
                  from
                    your
               lips—
            i can see a
          red hourglass
         body caressed in

black sauntering on
the cornered Keams of
your mouth's ravine—
Diné Bizaad—
dye—
i
n
g
the wool
over our eyes
with wet words
igniting images
abruptly disrupt—
i
n
g
the
stand
still
silence
of an
English—
colored
word
wilted
in the
whirlwind
of my father's
breath strokes
refining the
rich niche
of storytelling

coloring images
            with words
                        that I can
                                                still
                        see in
            flash—
es!

*Zoey Yazzie is a Diné Storyteller originally from Black Mesa and cur-
rently living in Durango. (y)az is Tódích'iinii—Bitterwater, born for
Áshįįhí—Salt, her maternal clan is Yé'ii Diné—Giant People, and her
paternal clan is Nóóda'í Dine'é Táchi'nii--The Ute People of the Red Run-
ning Into Water.*

I Bet You're a Good Husband

Tom Andes

We're sitting at the bar in the Monte Carlo Steakhouse, in Albuquerque, when the guy tells me about it. He tells me the Great Man—my father himself—once sat in his living room. Must've been back in eighty-four, he says.

"Eighty-four," I say. "No shit?"

I was nine years old in 1984, living with my mom on that quarter-acre lot she owned in Arcata, California. Back then we were living off government cheese, along with whatever vegetables she could grow in that patch behind the trailer. And that was before she got the cancer, back when things were good.

"I think so. Sometime around there, anyway. Eighty-four or eighty-five." He gives a self-deprecating little laugh, amused by his failing memory, the 40 years that have passed since then.

"You a country singer, too?" I say.

He's in a black leather jacket, jeans. He runs his finger around the rim of his rocks glass. He's drinking whiskey neat. His hand shakes, whether from age or from alcoholism, who knows.

"I play," he says, "but not like your dad did. I dabble. But I do other people's songs. I don't write them. It's a special gift your father had, writing all those songs."

I have to stop myself from throwing up, or from laughing in his face. Yeah, my old man wrote songs, seven or eight albums' worth. God knows how many more in the vault. He was a bona fide Texas troubadour, buddies with Guy Clark and Rodney Crowell, a mentor to Steve Earle, to Townes, the original junkie poet, with his Travis picking and his gravel voice a quarter-tone flat.

He was also a no-account son of a bitch who never did nothing for my mama, not even after he'd stuck it in her without a rubber and made her swell up like a pod full of peas.

"Yeah." I sip Bacardi and Diet Coke. "He was quite the writer."

If I sound bitter, well, the guy's just too over the moon talking about my father, too starstruck talking to the Great Man's daughter to notice it.

"What about you?" he says. "Do you sing? Do you play?"

Give him credit for that. Most people, it doesn't occur to them to ask, like they can't imagine I might've inherited the old man's gift, since I'm a woman. I don't blame people. That's how it is living in his shadow, a shadow that gets longer, the more time he's been dead and gone.

"I guess I'm a dabbler, too," I say. The guy nods, giving me a look like isn't that nice, us two dabblers sitting at the bar in a restaurant in the South Valley.

"I'm Rodger." He holds out his hand, still with that tremor, his eyes watery, like he's spent half the night crying, or like something's wrong with his tear ducts.

"I'm Candy."

It's short for Candace. Given name is Angela, like the Stones song, "Angie." My daddy was a big fan. But I stopped using that a long time ago.

His skin is cool, and it feels like parchment. If he's like half the men my daddy knew, all those road dogs and barstool prophets who turned their laments about women into song, I know what's coming next, and he'll put his hand on my knee. But he sips his drink and turns back toward the bar, something about him radiating what I can only call common decency.

"I bet you're a good husband," I say. "A good father."

Something goes out of his face. "I lost my wife a few years ago." And when I apologize, he holds up his hand, cutting me off. "It's okay. No way you could have known."

"I'm sorry anyway," I say.

In the mirror behind the bar, we sit with that, this graying, eighty-ish man my daddy's age, and me, a fifty-year-old woman, long past the age where men notice me on the street, so maybe it would've been a relief if he'd made a pass.

But no, I'm glad he didn't.

"You live around here?" It's something to say.

"Down the street." He gestures with his glass. "It's nice to get out at night and see people. What about you?"

I gesture at the outside world, pointing in the direction I think is south. It's easy to get turned around in here. The place doesn't have any doors or windows, and the ceilings are low, like we're in a cave. Across the room, there's a poster signed by that guy with the spiky hair who does that TV show, *Diners, Drive-ins, and Dives*.

"I live close, too." If he wasn't so decent, if decency wasn't oozing out of his skin like oil, I'd worry he might take that as an invitation. I hold my glass up and signal the bartender for another drink. I'll let Rodger pay for it, sure. "Thanks." I don't even mind when he leans over and pats my hand, paternal, affectionate.

He nods at the bartender. "Please." He'll have another, too. A waitress glides past with a couple plates on her arm. "You ever eat here," he says. "Ever try the food?"

"Once or twice, when someone else is paying. Place is a little rich for my blood."

A look is on his face, and maybe it's concern, like he's worried the Great Man's daughter is whoring herself out for a ribeye with a loaded baked potato. "It's very good."

"I don't eat out much," I say.

"Well, if you ever want to come sometime, I'll take you, my treat." And he raises that fresh drink to his lips, hand trembling, so he has to crane his neck.

"Do you mean that?" I don't want him to see it, but I might cry. It's the nicest thing anyone's said to me in a while.

"Of course I mean that," he says.

I'm a vegetarian, I tell him. "But I don't care. We can sit at one of the booths in the back. I'll have a loaded baked potato with sour cream and green chile."

They put green chile on everything around here.

I really am a vegetarian. Mostly, anyway. Hard not to be when you grew up abandoned by your daddy on a commune in Northern California living off handouts and what you could grow in your garden.

"It's a plan," Rodger says.

"How did you end up meeting my daddy, anyway? Did you work in music?"

He's looking at himself in the mirror behind the bar, his face as pale and gray as a statue between the rows of bottles. "I was a consultant, and I worked in politics for years. But I had a friend who played bass. He played in your daddy's band."

Who didn't? My old man traveled the country by Greyhound, playing with pickup bands, whatever musicians he could put together at the last minute when he blew through town. That was part of being a turnpike troubadour, that mythology, that cult he created. He lived for his art. But nobody talks about what that means for your family, the people who depend on you.

"That's nice for your friend." I sip my Bacardi and Diet Coke, the ice bumping my teeth. I need work done, a couple crowns, but good luck paying for that, with what I have to live off.

Rodger sounds like he's reminiscing, wistful, traipsing down memory lane, taken up with the romance of it all. "Troy did a couple tours with him, a few West Coast runs. But he had a family, wife and kids, so he decided he couldn't commit. Couldn't live the lifestyle in that way."

"That was good of him." I don't try to keep the bitterness out of my tone. What do I care? What I know about my old man, the only thing worse than him leaving my mama would've been if he'd stayed.

Rodger nods, like I've said something wise.

"Troy was a good man," he says.

"They're in short supply."

"What about you?" he asks. "What brings you to these parts of the world?"

Funny thing about Albuquerque, something I noticed when I first blew through here 25 years ago. For a city of over a million, no one thinks they're hot shit for living here, and they talk it down, like it's a backwater, the middle of nowhere. And it's true, we're out here in the desert, six hours from anyplace you'd want to be, except maybe Santa Fe, and who would want to be there?

"I don't know. I came through a couple times, back in the day, and one of those times, I stayed. I guess it always spoke to me."

Rodger's nodding. Half the people who end up here have a version of the same story. Maybe the same thing happened to him.

"Land of Enchantment," he says.

That's the state motto, which they put on the license plates, along with the chile peppers, red and green.

"Land of entrapment," I say, and he raises his eyebrows, making an expression like he hasn't heard that joke before, like it isn't a joke everyone makes.

"It's a good place," he says, somewhat defensively.

Good. I'm beginning to think everything is good to Rodger.

"It's all right," I say. "I mean, it's a place like any other."

He nods.

When he climbs off his barstool, I worry that he's going to fall, and I reach for his elbow to catch him. Somehow, we've ended up staying till closing, and the bartender brings our tickets, Rodger's check and mine, both of them on those little plastic trays.

"I've got these," Rodger says. I protest, but he waves me away.

"You don't have to do that," I say.

On the TV, they have one of those postgame shows, *Inside the NBA*, talking about the basketball that just ended. The bartender looks like he wants to throw me out, like he thinks I'm a working girl, scamming this old man, selling my ass.

"I know I don't," Rodger says, "but I want to. It's the least I can do, after all your family, all your old man's music, has done for me."

I feel weird about it, but when he pulls out that wallet, as fat and juicy as one of those ribeye steaks, I decide I'm okay with it.

He lays down a silver American Express card, which has his name on the front, Rodger Smith, and slides it across the bar. The bartender takes it. He's a graying guy with a trimmed beard and tattoos up and down his forearms. He's still giving me the stink-eye.

Rodger nods, with an expression of generosity so obvious, it makes me angry. Like he's the tooth fairy sticking a quarter under a kid's pillow. Then he turns and walks down the hall toward the bathrooms, those nice, pressed Levi's hanging off his hips, wobbling, so he must've been drinking before I showed up.

And Jesus, so help me, it would be better if he'd made a pass, if he did think I was selling it, because then I wouldn't have to feel so bad.

But the worst part is that he's good. Nice. Just a decent man mourning his wife.

Time passes, and Rodger's not back from the can. I know how it is, the way it ends for all these poor fools: they spend half their lives sticking it in every piece of chicken they come across, but they all end up in the same place, propping themselves up against the wall behind the john in a bar, trying to squeeze those last few drops out so they don't wet themselves when they zip up.

And I swear to you that I didn't plan this. I only do it because the opportunity presents itself. The bartender comes back and lays that tray with the silver AmEx card next to Rodger's half empty rocks glass. He gives me another look, like he still thinks I'm peddling pussy, and leans across the bar, breathing a mouthful of garlic at me.

"Don't come back in this place," he says. "Not if you know what's good for you."

Someone shouts from the back. Dishware clatters. He turns, ducking back through the doorway by the register. A calendar and an old school timeclock with timecards are on the wall.

He makes a point of leaving the card under the bar where I can't reach it, giving me a warning look as he walks back to the kitchen.

The dining room's empty, bus tubs on the tables, all that wood paneling and a bunch of faded posters on the walls. Likely this place hasn't changed since my daddy's day.

Hell, maybe my daddy ate here when he was passing through, on someone else's dime.

It doesn't take much. I belly up to the bar, standing on my tiptoes, lean across, and there's that silver credit card on a tray. I snatch it, walk out the door.

I walk fast down Atrisco, past the park and the baseball field.

Under the broken streetlights, someone's sleeping in the bus stop, and there's glass shattered by the curb, reflecting the starlight, like a detail my daddy might've put in a song.

When I get to the trailer, the door's locked, so I rattle it. Then I start kicking it.

"Sage." I'm pounding on the door. Inside the dogs are going crazy. "Open up, goddammit, right this second."

The kid's lazy, just like his old man, and it takes him a couple minutes.

"Hey, Mom." He wipes his nose.

I cuff him on the back of the head. Kid's 23, lives at home, a deadbeat.

"Put some clothes on," I tell him. He's still in his PJ's. "We're going to the Walmart."

"They're closed," he says.

In their crate, Zinnia and Pumpkin are going crazy, Zinnia snarling at the bars of the kennel cage, Pumpkin jumping and acting like a big dog, like she does.

I give the crate a kick, which quiets the dogs.

"Closed?" I sit on the couch.

I'd forgotten even the Superstores close at nine now.

"Since the pandemic. Ain't none of them open twenty-four hours, and it's a quarter of eleven."

"Shut up." I need time to think.

"What is it? What's wrong?"

He's standing by the door. Outside, a car drives past slowly on Atrisco, maybe Rodger or that bartender from the Monte Carlo looking for me, maybe just someone who's had a few, being careful on the drive home.

"Ran into an old friend of your grandfather's," I say, "is all."

"Is everything okay?"

He's a good kid, and he doesn't deserve this.

Maybe none of us deserve this.

"It's fine," I say. There's a 24-hour Allsup's off Isleta, and I decide I'm going there to get as many groceries, as many cans of beans and bags of potato chips as I can before Rodger cancels his card, if he hasn't already. "Just go back to bed."

In the back of the trailer is an old Yamaha guitar, frets busted halfway off the neck, the neck bowed from the heat, and it falls over when I pull my sweatshirt, a hoodie, out from underneath it. It's been ages since I played the damn thing, anyway.

"Hang tight." I grab my keys, the set we share. I rub Sage's head on the way out, messing up his hair. "I'll be back soon, with a little gift from your granddad."

Tom Andes wrote the detective novel Wait There Till You Hear from Me (*Crescent City Books,* 2025). His stories have appeared in Best American Mystery Stories 2012, Best American Mystery and Suspense Stories 2025, *and* The Best Private Eye Stories of the Year 2025. *A recent transplant to Albuquerque, he has immersed himself in the country and Americana music scene, touring Arizona, New Mexico, and Colorado, performing solo and with several bands. He is also a freelance editor. Southern Crescent Recording Co. re-released his acclaimed EPs on vinyl under the title* The Ones That Brought You Home *in 2025. He can be found at tomandes.com.*

Night Train with Cigarette

Lawrence Blair Goral

"I never paid a tax," the old man says,
Cups his hand round a match
Guttering in the wind of motion.

He lights and draws,
The train on weary tracks jolting us in synchrony,
Hammering flesh and bone.

The handrolled cigarette flares, etching deeper
The crags and crevices of his life-carved face,
Then fades.

"Oh, sure, sales tax on wine, maybe," he amends,
"But that don't count."
He breathes a plume of smoke, the night whipping it clear.

Hot wind spirals through the empty boxcar.
Outside, night spreads endless across the Utah flats
Where corpses of salt-encrusted trains rise
And pass, wrecked and ghostly in moonlight.

The car leans one way, leans again the other.
"Shit rails," he explains. "Shit shocks. Same as them,"
Gesturing with the cigarette through the wide door at the parallel
derelicts,
Warnings of our possible demise.

Somewhere, another state behind, the rampant blaze
Of casinos has dimmed to memory.

I still smell the wine on his breath and taste it on my tongue,
But the empty bottle sailed onto the desert an hour past.
Nor did we hear it shatter: the night swallowed it whole.

"And you," he says to me, "how come you ain't in school
Or workin in some damn office?"
"Too many walls," I say, trying to sound
Half as weathered as him. "Too many rules."
He laughs a wheezing laugh, because I am transparent as glass.

"All you upright citizens," he says, "lookin down your noses at me
Cause I'm drunk half the time, dirty most of the time,
And the rest of the time just fuckin poor."

He nods knowingly, flicks the meteor of his cigarette butt
Out into the rumbling night,
Silvering toward a jagged dawn above the distant Rockies.
"No, I never paid a tax," he says again.
"But then, *I* never gave a nickel to a war."

Writing has been Lawrence Blair Goral's through-line in a varied and eclectic life. He has been a zookeeper, a bookkeeper, a waiter, a construction worker, a field worker, and a photo studio manager. After a 20-year career as a technical editor, he and his wife retired to Bayfield, Colorado—cats included.

Lockdown

Jamie Nielsen

I've never driven to a middle school to sign a child out during a lockdown. This is the first time. I came for my son, who messaged:

there was a stabbing in the building we are in lockdown for the rest of the day can you pick me up

I wonder whether the woman at the front office will be angry. I imagine her saying things like: *We ask that parents wait to be notified!* and *We ask that you not impede the work of the police!*, broadcasting my selfishness for thinking only of my son, for compounding the problem, and, I'm ashamed to admit, for parking in a wheelchair-accessible space because there was nowhere else, I swear, between all the cars wedged in at crazy angles, halfway up berms of compacted winter snow.

But two women are holding the front doors open, speaking softly. "How are you it's down the stairs and to your left *please* have your photo ID ready." The building smells exactly the same as the public schools of my childhood: disinfectant, pencil shavings, chewing gum, locker room, gym shoes, and a whiff of cafeteria food.

People stand in line quietly, waiting for their turn at the front office window and watching for their child to emerge from a set of heavy double doors. They hug and make hushed phone calls. A man pulls a cart through the lobby, loaded with bottled water for the students. According to "shelter in place" protocols, the kids have to stay in their classrooms—for hours sometimes—behind more doors, with paper taped over the windows to hide any sign of life inside. A pulse of movement or warmth, a telltale flicker of light.

Next to me a woman sits on a metal chair, holding a toddler in her arms. Her little girl is in footie pajamas, curls sleep-pressed to one side of her head, sitting perfectly still, taking everything in.

When my son started middle school, he began asking us to knock before coming into his room. Suddenly here was Puberty and Personal Space, and a deep aversion to Family Game Nite. His dad and I became "cringey."

"Why can't you just please knock first?" he asked, understandably aggrieved. "You never *knock*." The hand-written sign he taped to his bedroom door read:

please knock. Dad and sister

+ mom

I crossed out "+ mom" on his sign, half joking, half serious, and wrote: "mom: you can come in." This, of course, was not well received.

My son, who is a hugger but does not allow public displays of affection now that he's 13, lets me wrap an arm around his shoulders as we hurry out of the school together. "Thanks for coming, Mom."

I tell him we need to stop for groceries on the way home. The sky is threatening another winter storm and we need a few provisions.

He senses a rare opportunity nested within the gravity of this day, a temporary shifting of priorities.

"Can we get Cocoa Puffs?" he asks.

As we hurry back out to the car with chocolate cereal, eggs, and a gallon of milk, I wonder about the kid in police custody and the kid in the ER, whether someone is with them now, asking if they're hungry and offering something from the vending machine, or, in the case of the kid at the hospital, something from that little refrigerator full of gelatin cups and apple juice at the nurses' station.

"You can talk to me about anything," I often tell my kids, and sometimes they do. I've banked everything I can remember from talks with my own parents, but these days I yearn to go home and sit with them again in the kitchen where I grew up, in Michigan, where the only drills we ever practiced at school were "fire" and "tornado." They advocated for my sister and me. They listened. When they died too young of cancer, I began to list a little to one side, as though I'd taken on water. The grief didn't capsize me completely, but there was an internal redistribution of weight with the heavy knowledge of our fragility on one side, and the awful lightness of their absence on the other.

As it turns out, this uneven load, this leaning, has permeated all my efforts at being a mother myself. I've become the kind of parent who doesn't leave anything unsaid, just in case our time is cut short. I try to make everything into a memory, take every opportunity to tell my son and daughter that I love them. I take too many pictures. I want them to store up these 10,000 small, daily offerings and keep them as a buffer against future scarcity, a breakwater in times of catastrophic grief, whatever form that may take.

My daughter was born in India with special medical needs. She left the orphanage to come with us to the United States when she was four and a half years old. She needs structure and affection and calorie-dense foods. Positive reinforcement, routines within routines, any excuse to bake together. She needs an advocate at school and with her doctors at the Cleft and Craniofacial Center at the children's hospital in Phoenix. She needs me to be there before surgeries and when she wakes up, holding her hand.

"Don't let go, Mom," she reminds me, and I pinky-promise. We have a system: One squeeze means "I love you." Two squeezes means "It's hurting me too much."

I told my children as little as possible about the biopsy, scheduled for two weeks from now. Three thin cores of tissue from my right breast. My daughter was severed from her birth mother. I don't want her to worry, even subconsciously, about losing her second one. The kids are unaware of the significance of any potential results. They have no idea what it is to witness the relentless advance of terminal illness in a loved one, or to right oneself in all the years following. The inherited menace of cancer casts long shadows; I'll do what I can to buy them a few more years of childhood in the sun.

In the car, on the way home from her elementary school, my daughter asks why I was so far back in the parent pick-up line, and I explain that I was late because I had to take Brother out of school for the day. There was a lockdown. Someone brought a knife and tried to hurt someone else. I'm slumped in the driver's seat, propped on my right elbow, listing again.

"In the *eye*?"

"No honey, not his eye."

"You mean, not the round kind of knife but the kind to cut chicken?"

"Something like that, but he's okay."

"We have a plan for lockdowns," she says, and proceeds to tell me, again, about locking the classroom door, staying very quiet and climbing out the window and running over the grass and into the trees as a last resort. We talk about this every time she has a practice drill. But this time she adds some new pieces, through the lens of a fourth-grader with a history of trauma who really, really loves her teacher, Ms. F.

". . . and Ms. F. has bricks in her closet," she tells me.

I decide not to ask how they plan to use those.

My daughter and I spend a lot of time in therapy together, un-learning certain "survival skills" from the first part of her life. For a long time it was hard for her to be in any room alone. She's hy-per-vigilant and afraid of the dark. It's taken some work for her to be able to ask to use the school bathroom when she needs it, and to go alone. We thought this was about not wanting to miss what's happening in class.

"If you're in the bathroom when the lockdown happens," she tells me, "you need to run as fast as you can to the closest classroom an' don't wait because the bad guy can find you in the bathroom an' once the classroom doors are locked they won't let you back in no matter what. No matter if he's comin' an' you're still in the hall an' knocking *please* let me in!"

"It sounds like you have a good plan in place," I say. I'm try-ing not to cry. I make an effort to straighten my spine, to rally my tendons and bones. Two hands, ten white knuckles on the steering wheel, I pull myself erect. Four-way stop. Signal on, turn right.

" 'An . . . Miz F will 'sacrifice herself for us'," she repeats.

I'm not even sure if she knows what that means.

Middle school is canceled the day after the lockdown. An email from the principal to parents and guardians reads:

". . . Our staff came together today to create a support plan. We began with a blessing, healing prayer and smudging . . . in partnership with Native Americans for Community Action (NACA)."

I call the school and ask who led the healing prayer and smudg-
ing—the cleansing with smoke from a bundle of sage. They give me
the name of Mr. D, a member of the Navajo Nation and a licensed
mental health counselor. He has an impressive list of degrees and
certifications next to his picture on the NACA website. Some I recog-
nize, like "Master of Science in Clinical Mental Health Counseling"
and "Cognitive Behavioral Therapy," but other things read more
like poems: "White Bison Wellbriety: Medicine Wheel/12 step."

Snow keeps falling in the weeks after the lockdown; there are
as many snow days as school days. My husband and I bend and
shovel until our backs ache, working in shifts, peeling off our coats
and sweaty layers. He tackles the heaviest chunks, deposited by city
snowplows like a wall of boulders at the end of the driveway. The
piles grow to five feet, then seven. I carve and re-carve a path to the
front door. My work is erased in a matter of hours, but it's the prin-
ciple of the thing. It's one kind of barrier I can break open.

I call Mr. D to let him know I'm going to be late getting to his
office. I'm shoveling, but it's going to take a while to get my car out.
No problem, my door is always open, he says. And it is. There are
hide drums along one wall, and rocks chosen and painted by chil-
dren as a part of their therapy. One rock is midnight blue, speckled
with a beautiful universe of tiny, white stars. Mr. D is a thoughtful,
quiet presence in this small room that doesn't feel small. There is
space for both of us, and all the people we carry with us. I choose a
chair and we talk about our families and the fresh, deep snow blan-
keting the mountain. We talk about what happened at the middle
school.

"Scared can go two ways: violence or compassion," he says, and
I think about the student who brought a knife in his backpack and

tried to jam it into someone else's abdomen. Instead, the knife cut deep into a skinny forearm, the only available shield in that desperate moment. I think about the scars, our human capacity to hurt each other, our capacity—proclivity even—for destruction. Mr. D offers me a box of tissues.

The day after the lockdown, he tells me, the teachers and staff sat in a circle—the shape of connection and safety—and were given space to breathe and cry. Mr. D played his flute, burned sage, and offered a prayer that the next day, when the students returned, the teachers would be able to expand their circle to cover them too. *And the woman at the front desk,* I think, *and the little sister in pajamas. And the water guy.*

As a child, Mr. D's father survived life in an Indian residential boarding school. Severed from his home and family, he was punished for practicing traditional Navajo rites of renewal and connection. I have learned, in therapy with my daughter, that we carry trauma in our bodies. It can change the structure and connectivity of our brains. In Mr. D's words, his dad had to "build a wall to protect himself" and it's still there today. When the family invites Mr. D's father to burn cedar with them or join in a sweat lodge, he always declines.

When the middle school called Mr. D on the day of the lockdown, he decided "to enter and give back," for everyone at the school, where over a quarter of the students are Native American, and for the whole community. Mr. D wants Native American youth "to see that it's okay, it's safe now" to openly practice traditional rites of healing without fear of persecution—one small step toward dismantling centuries of intergenerational trauma.

"Each of us carries a legacy of burdens," Mr. D says. He understands about listing and leaning, and the danger of capsizing. "Internal balance, or *hózhó*, requires owning your weaknesses and hurts." In other words, vulnerability. One path to healing and resilience.

Mr. D lights a bundle of sage and I lean in to the cleansing smoke, elbows on my knees, breathing and listening to his kind words. The juniper sage smells like home. My parents' kitchen is not there, but I smell our wood fire on winter nights and other familiar things: pine sap and muddy earth under melting snow. The steady creep toward the relief of another spring, and the blessing of lengthening days. I drive home thinking about courage (Mr. D's) and vulnerability (mine, everyone's).

The day of the biopsy, school is canceled again and the snow is accumulating so quickly that Radiology calls and asks me to come early: "We don't want to delay your procedure, but for everyone's safety we need to close early." My husband rides along so he can drive me home. We strain forward in our seatbelts, squinting into the whiteout, trying to make out the contours of the road. I told him I could handle this myself, but I'm suddenly glad he's here.

He keeps vigil in the empty waiting area. I hold this in my mind as I strip off my warm clothes and pull on an enormous, faded hospital gown. Down the hall, outside another set of heavy double doors, he knows I'm in here.

I imagine I'm holding my daughter's hand, only this time I'm on the table and she's leaning over me. I clench my teeth and squeeze once.

That night I tape a peace offering on my son's bedroom door, a replacement sign:

Please Knock for Permission to Enter.

(Mom: you can knock if you need a hug.)

One week passes, then two, and he doesn't take it down. He keeps his door closed but not locked, since I committed to knocking and trying not to linger.

I don't have any words, after the doctor calls, for "fibro adenoma, completely benign," but I find myself knocking and then standing outside his bedroom door, smiling and unsure of what to do with my hands. I hear the rumble of his desk chair rolling closer. He opens the door, still seated, eyes on his laptop.

"Guys, hang on a sec." He's playing multiplayer Minecraft with a group of friends, but he turns from the screen and asks: "Mom. Do you need a hug?"

Jamie Nielsen is an ecologist and former U.S. Peace Corps volunteer. She lives and writes in Flagstaff with her husband, two children, and their rescue dog, Rainy. Her essays appear in The Sunlight Press*, the* Arizona Authors' Association Arizona Literary Magazine 2021*,* Cleaver Magazine*, and* Empty House Press*. She's currently polishing her memoir manuscript and loves writing essays for "Swammits & Mash Tippy-Toes"(Sandwiches and Mashed Potatoes): jamie677.substack.com.*

Sunrise by the Blue Lake

Irene I. Blea

the golden glint of sunrise emerges from between the mountains
where the sacred Blue Lake is the first to receive it
beyond it live women and their sons of fire
women of the blue corn
their daughters attuned to the hummingbird's song

brave hearts beat
guardians of the pueblo
rich not with gold
with the treasure of purple honor
wisdom and oneness

history is woven by the trees
stone and spirit
beside the blue lake
in secret I speak with the moon

whisper with the wind among the pines

they remember my name
remind me to keep balanced
honor the dead, they say
their spirits walk amongst us
visit us as we dance

present in the clay of our fired pottery
in the blue corn I planted
is the memory of the souls
of my many ancient grandmothers

Irene I. Blea, a native of New Mexico, has a Ph.D. in Sociology from the University of Colorado-Boulder, and has published textbooks for university classroom use, popular and academic articles, and novels. Her poetry book, **Dragonfly,** *offers guidance and transformation. She first read her poetry during the 1970s civil rights movement.*

The Storyteller

Caroline Brown

Anna raced to her dorm, where her roommates were crowded around the radio.

"Who shot them?" she asked nervously. Jill replied, "I think it was the National Guard."

"No, no, no," Anna mumbled. "Why?"

The girls in the room shook their heads. "Nobody knows."

The photos and details of the Kent State shootings on the front page of the next day's *Rocky Mountain News* were so horrific that Anna started packing her car.

"Where are you going?" Jill asked.

"Home," Anna responded.

"We're in the middle of finals! They'll probably start classes again before the week is over. There's no reason for the Guard to come here."

Anna replied, "You don't know that for sure."

"Are you coming back?"

"No."

"Tell me again where your grandparents live."

"McElmo Canyon, in southwest Colorado."

Anna hugged Jill and started down the stairs. "Wait," Jill called out. "What about The Good and The Ugly?"

They'd bought three little green turtles with painted designs on their shells from Woolworth's when they first became roommates in 1967. Jill named them The Good, The Bad, and The Ugly. The Bad died, but The Good and The Ugly had adjusted to dorm life.

"Okay, I'll make room for them."

"Thank you," the turtles said in unison. Anna smiled back at them.

As Anna began the 400-mile drive to her grandparents' farm, she was still wearing the t-shirt she'd put on the day before. It said MAKE LOVE - NOT WAR. When she arrived at the farm, Magpie called out from the branch of the cottonwood tree, "Anna's home!"

It had been two years since Anna had left her college campus and moved home to McElmo Canyon. When she first got back, there were several weeks left of late calving and lambing season, so she stayed busy helping neighbors. One rancher down the road had a dozen first-calf heifers that decided 1:00 a.m. was the best time to calf out.

Being back in her natural environment had slowly restored Anna's sense of well-being. She took her grandfather's mare for unhurried rides into side canyons and along the creek bed where the wild apricot trees blossomed. She read as her grandmother wove tapestries on an old floor loom.

She was working on a macramé piece when her grandmother handed her the letter. "Oh my god," Anna exclaimed. "This is from my college roommate."

"Well, it probably wasn't easy for this letter to find you, addressed like it is," Grandma muttered.

"Maybe someday there'll be an easier way for people to find each other when they've lost touch," Anna said as she tore open the letter.

"Maybe," Grandma answered.

Anna quickly replied to Jill's letter, and a few weeks later they met in Santa Fe. Anna's t-shirt read WILLIE NELSON - OUTLAW COUNTRY. After hugs, they began catching up with each other's lives. Jill worked in a bookstore and was enamored with the Santa Fe vibe. She talked so fast that Anna could hardly keep up.

Finally out of breath, Jill asked Anna what she was up to.

"I'm taking classes at Fort Lewis College in Durango and I should have my degree and teaching certification next year. Oh, by the way, Good and Ugly are doing well."

"What?" Jill squealed. "I can't believe they're still alive."

"A few weeks after I got home, I was helping Doc Adams vaccinate and deworm the horses. For some reason we started talking about reptiles and I told him about Good and Ugly. Doc said he wasn't a reptile veterinarian, but he did know about red-eared sliders because thousands of them had been sold in the 1960's. Many of the surviving turtles were released in ponds and streams all over the US. They're considered invasive because they compete with native species for food and habitat."

Anna continued, "My grandfather and I built special enclosures for them in the garden. We bring them inside in October where they have a hibernation environment in the basement."

The next morning, Jill was eager to show Anna the Museum of Indian Arts and Culture. As they wandered about, Anna was drawn to a special exhibit. The curator came over and nodded at Anna.

"So there you are," he said. "The Storytellers told me you might come by today."

"What exquisite beings," Anna murmured.

"These figurines are called Storytellers," the young man explained. "They physically represent the oral practice of storytelling and how it gives eternal life to Pueblo culture. Many of the Pueblo Tribes have started creating their own version of the Storyteller again."

"Again?" asked Anna.

"Here, read this pamphlet. It explains the Storytellers' history better than I can. I'm from Acoma Pueblo, but the people at Cochiti are our relatives."

Anna could hear the Storytellers in the exhibit whispering among themselves as she read the pamphlet.

In 400 AD, these figurines were an integral part of the Pueblo culture. Storyteller pottery disappeared between 1500 and 1875, when the first missionaries denounced the making of figurative clay pieces.

Pueblo artists began making Storytellers again in the late 1800s. The first contemporary Storyteller pottery was created by Helen Cordero of Cochiti Pueblo in 1964.

Each Storyteller portrays an elder, often in traditional attire, surrounded by children. They symbolize the passing down of wisdom, knowledge, and cultural heritage from one generation to the next.

Storyteller pottery figurines are hand-coiled and shaped with natural clays that are gathered from the earth. These pottery pieces are then fired and intricately hand painted.

Anna felt her pulse accelerate. "Can I go to Cochiti Pueblo?"

"Of course," the young man answered. "It's about 40 miles south of here."

Anna told Jill she was leaving, but that they would get together again soon. Jill only nodded. She knew something important was happening for Anna.

Anna followed the directions to the turnoff. "Now what?" she wondered aloud. "Turn here," a faint voice responded.

Anna slowly drove past the homes until she saw the sign *Potteries for Sale.*

"Stop here," the voice said.

Anna got out of her truck and bent down to pet the welcoming pup. "*Guw'aadzi*, hello" the puppy yapped. Anna smiled and knocked on the door.

"Come in, come in," the old man called out. "We've been waiting for you. She's ready."

Anna entered the home. Newspaper was laid out on a card table. Sitting in the middle of the table, surrounded by jars of mineral pigments, was a small, freshly-painted Storyteller figurine.

The old man's wife came into the room, wiping her hands on an apron covered with her floured handprints. Anna hadn't uttered a word, but she finally said, "I think you're expecting someone else. I was just driving by and saw the sign in your window."

"No, we've been waiting for you," the woman answered.

"Did someone from the museum call you?" Anna asked.

"No, *K'uyaw*," the old man replied. "No one called us. We don't have a phone."

"Come in the kitchen. Come eat," his wife said.

No sooner were they seated than she pushed a bowl of posole towards Anna. She tore off a piece of fresh-baked bread and put it on Anna's plate.

"This smells delicious. What kind of bread is this?" Anna asked.

"It's traditional pueblo bread made from white flour, lard, and salt," the woman explained. "It begins as a large rounded loaf that's divided into sections before it's baked in the *horno*."

"Here at Cochiti," the woman continued, "we split ours into small sections so it's easier to tear apart. We call it elephant toes. The Zuni make larger sections they call bear claws or Dolly Parton."

"Why Dolly Parton?" Anna inquired.

The old man laughed in the next room. "Because the round portions are so big."

Storyteller had resided on a shelf in the farmhouse for over twelve years. Anna often eavesdropped on the intriguing conversations between Storyteller and the ever-changing parade of barn cats that declared themselves as house cats.

Anna knitted by the fire one winter evening wearing her I'M NOT SOCIALLY AWKWARD - I JUST REALLY LIKE CATS sweatshirt. Her grandparents had already gone to bed. The quiet was interrupted when Old Cat said, "Tell us a story."

Storyteller spoke of a young Cochiti boy who was forced to go to boarding school. The instructor told him to forget the stories he'd heard from his grandparents about the bear, deer, insects, and other creatures that talked to the Cochiti people. He was told those stories were not true. This made the boy very sad.

A few days later the instructor told the class about missionaries who had a book with a story about a snake that talked to a woman holding an apple in a beautiful garden. The boy was confused.

One day the boy's people came and took him home to Cochiti. He grew up to be a fine man who made small Storytellers for all of his friends and relatives.

"Good story," said Old Cat.

"Good story," said Owl from the branch of the cottonwood tree.

Driving home after a summer solstice-birthday celebration spent camping with friends in Echo Basin, Anna saw the unmistakable shape of an injured dog on the side of the road. She slammed on the brakes and quickly ran to the dog. "Oh, sweetheart. What happened to you?"

"I don't know," the frightened dog answered.

"I'll call Doc Adams," Anna said in a comforting voice. She carefully lifted the distraught dog into her truck and stopped at the first pay phone she saw. Maybe someday, she thought, people will have better access to phones.

It was nearly dusk when Anna pulled up to Doc's clinic. After he examined the pup, Doc said she would need to stay overnight, and he would operate on her leg the following day.

"Okay." Anna said. "What kind of dog do you think she is?"

"I'm surprised at you, Anna. You've lived here all of your life. I thought for sure you'd recognize this breed."

Anna felt a little embarrassed and shrugged.

"She's a Western Bitsa," Doc said.

Anna shrugged again.

"They're common out here," Doc chuckled. "She's a bits of this, and a bits of that."

In spite of the late hour and her concern for the dog, Anna laughed.

"We'll need to fill out some paperwork, but let's start with her name," Doc said.

"Her name is Bitsa," Anna replied.

July 12, 1988

Dear Jill:

I hope you and Henry and the kids are doing OK.

Our phones are out again. And, I just hate paying those expensive long distance charges. I wanted to let you know that my grandfather passed away last month. It was a shock, but my grandmother is doing pretty good. She said that everyone wants to go to heaven, but no one wants to die.

He was 90. Other than when he was in the military, he lived on this farm his whole life. He's buried in the Farrell family cemetery plot on the farm.

I'm looking forward to seeing you and your family before summer's over.

Love,

Anna

A few years before he'd passed away, Anna's grandfather had

told her how her great-grandfather Joseph Farrell, back in the late 1880s, had homesteaded their 200 acres and acquired adjudicated water rights. He was one of the first ranchers to irrigate in McElmo Canyon, but he complained about how complicated the water rights, ditch rights, and irrigation could be. Joseph said there was so much red tape you could wrap a Christmas tree with it.

But, he'd persevered and married his childhood sweetheart. When Joseph bought his first 20 head of Hereford cattle, he registered a small brand, a sideways F. He said the larger shaped brands were unnecessarily cruel to the cattle during fire branding and took longer to heal.

Doc Adams pulled up in his mobile veterinary truck. Bitsa greeted him with her usual excitement, sniffing for the treat Doc always brought for her. Anna was wearing her JUST A GIRL WHO LOVES CHICKENS AND ALPACAS t-shirt.

"So, you're going into the alpaca business."

"I'm starting with three, primarily for their wool, but I'm already so smitten with them that I'll probably increase the herd. Are you familiar with alpaca care?"

"All us old guys are trying to keep pace with the evolving world of livestock," Doc replied. "I've been to a couple of work seminars on llamas and alpacas. I was even at a training last month for AI with Angus bulls. That's getting more popular on the Front Range, but I suspect the ranchers around here might be interested in AI at some point."

"AI?" Anna asked.

"Artificial Insemination. There's no other procedure with those two letters, so I don't think the abbreviation AI will be confused with anything else."

"Probably not," Anna agreed.

When Anna's grandmother delegated the farm decisions to her,

Anna had the alfalfa plowed under and put in orchard grass that didn't use as much water. The three acres of lavender that were successfully cultivated proved to be a solid business venture. It was drought tolerant, an excellent pollinator plant, and there was never a shortage of buyers.

Anna flipped the 1994 calendar page. "Geez," she sighed. "It's already August. School will be starting soon. I can't believe I've been teaching third grade for twenty years. Ten more years and I can retire with my PERA pension."

"*Hin'a, Dawaa dza,*" replied Storyteller. "You work hard."

The phone rang as Anna was sitting on the porch, shelling peas and listening to one of Magpie's stories. She was wearing her new t-shirt, LOVE, PEACE, AND NAVAJO TACOS.

"Farrell Family Farms," Anna answered.

"I was sorry to hear about your grandmother," Jill said. "She was an incredible woman."

"Yeah, she was. Lived to be 102. She was born in 1899 and died in 2001. She lived during three different centuries as well as the first and second millennia."

Anna continued, "A few days before Grandma went into hospice, she gave me a quilt made from my old t-shirts. It was the last project she worked on. My favorite block is the t-shirt design with the cowgirl on a bucking horse that says CHEYENNE FRONTIER DAYS 1969."

Jill giggled. "That was one great weekend!"

After hanging Christmas lights around the windows, Anna built a fire and stooped down to cuddle with Old Cat.

"I reckon it's time for me to go see Doc Adams," Old Cat wheezed in a muffled voice.

"Are you sure?" Anna asked.

Old Cat nodded.

The next day Anna held Old Cat in her arms as Doc prepared the sodium pentobarbital. "You know, Doc, I've had a lot of animals in my life, so that means I've lost a lot of animals. I thought by now this part would be easier."

"No, Anna," Doc said quietly. "This doesn't get easier. It actually becomes more difficult the older you get."

As Doc gently injected Old Cat she looked at Anna, exhaled, and said, "See you later, alligator."

"After a while, crocodile," Anna whispered with tears in her eyes.

Five years into retirement, Anna was busier than at any time in her life. Jill's grandson had created a website for Farrell Family Farms' wool business, and it was thriving. Anna contracted out the 100-acre hay production, which continued to be the backbone of the farm. The orchards required the most labor and time, but each acre of fruit trees produced an adequate profit. The seasonal farm workers continued the never-ending battle keeping tamarisk and Russian olive out of the irrigation ditches.

Jill surprised Anna with a 65th birthday party at the farm on the summer solstice. Jill's family, farm workers, friends, former students, and even retired Doc Adams attended. Anna wore her GRAY HAIR – DON'T CARE t-shirt. After cake and ice cream, Jill asked Anna to give a speech. Anna took a deep breath and said, "Time really does fly when you're happy."

As she slowly walked through the Arriola Cemetery gate, Anna shivered in the cold. The headstone read:

MICHAEL (DOC) ADAMS

1944 – 2020

"Oh, Doc," Anna said. "There was a vaccine on the horizon. If only . . ." But Anna didn't finish the sentence.

"You were such a good friend. You told me about the Montezuma Orchard Restoration Project. That was a game-changer for the farm. Planting the grapevines was your idea, and I'm still selling to local wineries. Every animal on the property loved you." Anna hesitated, then quietly said, "So did I."

Anna threw on her I READ BANNED BOOKS t-shirt and picked the April 23, 2025 *Cortez Journal* up off the table. A photo on the front page highlighting people at the Hands Off rally caught her attention. Anna recognized the sign she was carrying, but her face appeared blurry in the photograph.

"I'll send Jill the newspaper link," Anna said as she glanced at Storyteller.

"When are you going to write your stories?" Storyteller asked. "It's time for you to begin a new chapter."

Anna smiled at Storyteller's play on words. "I don't have any stories. I'm pretty sure stories consist of a beginning, a middle and an end, in addition to a plot. Also," Anna continued, "I think there's supposed to be a good guy and an adversary."

Storyteller patiently replied, "No, *K'uyaw*. Your experiences are your stories."

"My experiences haven't been all that exciting," Anna replied. "I don't know who would want to read my stories."

Storyteller softly spoke, "Storytellers, like farmers, plant seeds without always knowing the outcome of the harvest."

After a lingering silence, Anna looked at Storyteller and said, "Hmmm. Maybe I'll give it a try."

"Maybe she'll give it a try!" chattered Magpie from the branch of the cottonwood tree.

Caroline Brown lives in Dolores with her husband, her dog, and a clay Storyteller figurine.

Seep 1

Linda Barnes

Deep in the shaded recesses
of sunbaked sandstone folds,
a seep hides in the dark.
Here gossamer-like wisps of moss
and delicate fern cling to a canyon wall,
scarcely visible, shielded from the searing desert heat.
Slivers of green nestle in a moist crevasse
radiant against the burnt orange rock.

Sentience glistens, sensual and wet,
thriving on a miniscule drip of water.
Seeping, sourced from deep within the earth,
leaking along the hairline of existence.
Weeping in private, hidden from sight.

Linda Barnes has lived on the Colorado Plateau for 25 years now after years in New York City as a midwife in one of the large city hospitals. After a 10-year stint with Indian Health Service on the Navajo Nation, she is now retired to continue exploring our beautiful Plateau with its canyons, mountains, streams and valleys.

An Ode to the Stray Messiah

Lawrence Blair Goral

The cat came to us dying, but he lived.

Our neighborhood, in the piñon-juniper woodland skirting the feet of the San Juans, hosts a moderately dispersed human population, but other residents abound. Deer, squirrels, rabbits, elk; coyotes, bobcats, foxes; not infrequently I follow mountain lion tracks on my morning walk. Sometimes the internet reports a bear sighting in the vicinity, though I've never come across any sign myself. A trio of bald eagles wintered on the ridge behind us, and in the summer prairie rattlesnakes emerge from burrows in our yard. It's a rich community, but not a kind one to the vulnerable or infirm.

The cat appeared to us out of the brush one random day when the nights were falling into single digits and puddles stayed frozen past noon: skeletal, near blind with pus and discharge, skulking and desperate. *Feral*, was my first thought—but when I approached he thrust his crusty head into my hand. I left to get him food and water and he followed me, as diligent as a well-trained dog. After we assembled a place for him in our garden shed, complete with blanket and heater, he still tried to follow me to the house, but I walked him back and pointed at the gapped door and he entered without me and took up his new abode as if it had always been his. As if he knew.

Thus he entered our lives.

Once in a great while, if you are fortunate, an entity—rare as a unicorn, bright and transitory as a shooting star—will touch you, and leave you forever changed. A gift, a fulcrum, perhaps a revelation. Entity, I say, because not all are human. Maybe, even—had we eyes to see and hearts to feel—most are not.

This is not the self-congratulatory story of adopting an unfortunate creature, but a reflection on the myriad lives we overlook. Thibault—the name we gave him, signifying *brave people*—exhibited extraordinary qualities from that first day, even beyond managing to survive one of the coldest spells of this Colorado winter. He, like only two other cats I've been privileged to know, transcends the normal limitations of his species. I've met a handful of dogs over the years that likewise rose above the conventional understanding of doghood.

I have even, I must acknowledge, encountered a few humans who merit inclusion in this transformative fraternity.

All these shine in memory.

Such beings are scattered like windborne seeds across cultures and centuries, intersecting lives by chance or some unfathomable design. Some become seers, prophets, dreamers and visionaries— even messiahs—while others fall on barren ground, where they lie unremarked and ultimately lost.

Time and timing, chance and serendipity, shape our destinies in ways we can never know. A momentary shift in our daily schedule and Thibault would have ended as a coyote's meal or a furred and flattened stain on the roadside, another passing casualty, insignificant as the rest. He was, in any event, no more than days from death when he found us.

A fluke; a chance encounter. What story would he tell if only he were able? What chain of circumstance or misfortune threw him onto this precipitous descent? Where had he journeyed, what had he endured? Clearly he had been loved once, or he'd not be so human-attuned; just as clearly, he had been somehow severed from that idyllic past, cruelly or casually or just circumstantially.

Something we can never know.

So one wonders—one must, unless one deliberately chooses not to—how many others? Not just thrown-away cats or dogs, but humans, too: how many children languishing in refugee camps; how many homeless, so easily dismissed as human flotsam; how many washed in the rising tide of mass migrations, flights from war or poverty or persecution or just a hostile sky or season; how many, subsumed in these hordes of the nameless wounded, carry that same spark, that same potential for extraordinary transcendence, as the stray cat who staggered half-blind and toothless into our quotidian existence—and transformed it?

Metaphor abounds and lessons surround us, an encroaching army of wisdom—if we listen, if we see. If we strive to penetrate beyond the disfigured skin; to discern, beneath our differences, our commonalities: deeper than race, gender, religion, nationality—deeper even than species.

Thibault looks into my eyes in a way most cats never do: as if there is a seeking, a reaching for communion. I look back, trying just as hard to connect. Likely I can't; likely some secret message must remain forever untransmitted, untranslated, interdicted by the gulf between species. But maybe, maybe, the real illumination rises in the attempt itself.

It's been some time since Thibault came to us. There have been multiple trips to his Durango veterinarian. He's still not well—still wheezing, still struggling—but he is improving. The vet tells us that there will never be a complete recovery, that in fact his condition is terminal, but we don't know, can't know, how long we'll have with him. That, of course, is the great uncertainty each of us must carry through every life, every relationship: the whims of fate and hazard. What we do know is that he has, in his quiet needful way, immeasurably enriched us.

So maybe, even in the darkest times, the fundamental lesson is this: that it will always be the smallest, most unremarked kindnesses, given or received, that sustain us.

Writing has been Lawrence Blair Goral's through-line in a varied and eclectic life. He has been a zookeeper, a bookkeeper, a waiter, a construction worker, a field worker, and a photo studio manager. After a 20-year career as a technical editor, he and his wife retired to Bayfield—cats included.

Ode to the Slow

Wendy Videlock

I've an affinity for ghosts, and so,
dwelling as we ghostly do, with the caw
and the screech and the piñon moon, where the freeze
and the thaw and the witness are
together alive and together entombed,
here on the edge of a high desert world
where all is stone, and all is sky,

here where an ancient sea surged forth
and slowly died, here where the ruins and the peaks
have changed their names to butte and bluff,
here where the Ute had slowed their feet
and harvested the piñon seed,
here where the reach of the canyon ends
or begins, or infers —like knowledge, it's always

a rapture or a bit of a blur— (one could soar on the wing
or fall in) — here where the rolling stone knows
the world is only made of sand, and the arc
is the mark of the fallen star,
here where the ghosts and the slopes are wan,
and empty of virtue and of sin, I lower a bridge,
and watch the morning fog roll in.

Wendy Videlock lives in Western Colorado. Her works appear widely. Wendy is a syndicated newspaper columnist and serves as Colorado's Western Slope Poet Laureate. Her books include Wise to the West *and the* Poetic Imaginarium. *A sense of place is the central impulse in her work.* "Ode to the Slow" *first appeared in* Hopkins Review.

Mannequin

donalee Moulton

Max is holding court. Admittedly, his throne is a wooden picnic table on my mother-in-law's flagstone patio, and the courtiers are a motley assortment of neighbors, family, and friends jostling for chile rellenos, Sour Red Ale, a place to sit, eat, and maybe, just maybe, let Max regale them with whatever anecdote tops his storyboard today.

There is a twenty-something at his elbow hanging on his every word. She's the niece of a neighbor, and she is no threat. There is always a twenty-something or a thirty-something, sometimes even a forty-something. There is always a cousin or a godchild or a sister. And they are no threat.

I'm the wife. I'm used to this. Truth is, I'm indifferent. Max is the anchor of Farmington's highest-rated six o'clock news broadcast. He has a lot of stories. Some of them are even true. He also knows how to tell a good story: resonance, pacing, eye contact.

My husband is not going anywhere but home to me. He may be

late arriving, and he may be weaving when he gets there, but he has a built-in homing device that has not failed him yet. Or me. I'm not worried about Max straying, or about Max ignoring me, or about Max making a fool of either of us

I'm worried about the dry cleaning.

I have a presentation tomorrow to the senior management team. Not an important presentation, certainly, nor a controversial one. Indeed, I doubt the findings I share will surprise anyone. But I want the people around that table to be impressed. I've planned what to say, and I've planned what to wear: a cream-colored Altuzarra maxi dress. It's comfortable and stylish. It's also a shade that shows every speck of dirt and debris.

I've taken care of this. The dress is at the dry cleaner. Dry cleaning is on Max's to-do list. To his credit, the dress arrived at Century Cleaners. Now it needs to make its way out, and Max is holding court.

I opt for a nudge. I bring a plate of nachos and dip to the table. I'm greeted with smiles and outstretched hands from almost everyone. Twenty-something pointedly ignores me. Max continues uninterrupted, so I interrupt.

"Another Sour Red?" Not my first rodeo.

Max stops. He looks up. Not his first rodeo either. "What will it cost me?"

"A trip down East 20th to the dry cleaner."

"That can wait till tomorrow."

"I have a presentation tomorrow."

"And you have other clothes."

Twenty-something titters. Max takes his empty glass and upturns it on the picnic table. The corn-chip crunching stops.

"You're right," I say. I smile. "I'll ask your mother to bring you some more cerveza." Laughter erupts around the table. Max grins. Twenty-something pointedly ignores me.

Max is right, screw the dry cleaning. I have more clothes. Nice clothes. Expensive clothes. Still, this was the outfit I had selected down to the shoes and accessories. The question should be: Do I go to the dry cleaner myself, or do I choose something else to wear?

Back in the kitchen I pour myself a lime and tonic. (I couldn't be bothered with the gin.) I'm sipping absently, nodding at my mother-in-law as if I'm hearing what she's saying. I replay the picnic table conversation. I replay similar conversations over the past sixteen years. I sip. I nod.

I have the answer.

I'm done.

I grab my purse and head for the door. My mother-in-law stops midsentence, I assume to pick her jaw off the talavera tiles. I'm out the door, car keys in hand. Two late-comers, Evan and Ada, are coming in as I go out.

"That bad?" they ask in unison.

"All's good." I'm telling the truth. "Just running a quick errand." I'm lying.

I'm in the car, the engine is humming, I'm reaching for the gearshift. It's now or never.

It's now.

I head east on San Juan, then north on Hutton. I have no idea where I'm going. I pull over at the first available spot. I need clothes, and I need a place to stay. I put the car back in gear and continue driving. First stop: home. En route I call the Courtyard and book a room for the evening. A suite. I don't usually splurge like this, but I deserve it.

Max will be holding court for another few hours. Mama will have refilled his drink by now and smiled pleasantly at twenty-something. I'm in no rush. I pack some clothes, work and otherwise. Enough to get me through to Thursday. Max has a broadcasters' conference in Chicago on Thursday. He will not miss that, and the house will be mine to do whatever I need to do.

Since I'm here, I decide to poke around in Max's computer. I'm not sure why, but the word "ammunition" rattles around in my brain. It takes me less than a minute to access his email. Nothing here at first glance. I write down the access info for later.

It takes me about three minutes to find the bank account. The bank account I didn't know existed.

Oh Max, you have been a bad boy.

I'm an investment banker with the biggest of the big four banks. (Everyone says the bank they work for is the biggest; mine really is.) I understand how money is moved. I know the process by which funds find their way into an account, and I know how to reverse that process. That's exactly what I do. Max will discover, eventually, that the money he's been siphoning off his paycheck into a separate account is no longer in that account.

I transfer the money to our joint account. That leaves a paper trail. The trail will end tomorrow when I withdraw the funds using a money order. Untraceable. I'll put my newfound money in my newly-opened account at First Financial. Look at me, embracing change.

To fuck with Max, I send an email to his HR department (Max, you really need stronger encryption) and request that his full paycheck go directly to our joint account. I also change the password on both accounts. It will take him a while to figure out what's going on.

I'm out of time. More than an hour has elapsed since I left my mother-in-law's, and my husband. I grab my overnight bag, my laptop, and the $600 bottle of Scotch, the one Max was saving for a special occasion. It's a win-win.

I'm in the car driving back toward Hutton when it occurs to me that the dry cleaner is only ten minutes away. Since I'm in the vicinity . . .

Century Cleaners is a mess. This is my first visit, and I wonder if it's always in this disarray. Perhaps this is why Max seems so reluctant to come here. Yellow "Caution: Do Not Enter" tape stretches from the left side of the main door all the way behind the front counter. The tape is keeping customers out of what looks like a small dressmaking disaster. There are hangers, racks, swaths of fabric, a file cabinet, and needle cases strewn across the floor. A mannequin lies on its side, its tripod base pointing toward the ceiling. Dust balls cling to the cotton torso.

The woman behind the counter sees my open mouth.

"We buy tailor shop. Fixing up. You want anything? All for sale."

I appreciate the brevity, and the explanation is somewhat reassuring. I shake my head in response to the sales pitch. "I'm here to pick up a dress." I hand over my slip.

It takes Brevity only a few seconds to return with my dress, and a gray suit that belongs to Max. Of course, I send things to the cleaner in batches. Brevity is looking at me curiously. I reach for my wallet, and my credit card. But first, I slide across a coupon. There is twenty percent off everything this month.

Brevity takes in the Altuzarra dress and the Tom Ford suit. She looks at me, then she looks at the coupon. I slide the coupon closer. Brevity gives me my clothes and my discount. I toss the suit in the disaster area on my way out.

The Courtyard is everything it claims to be. As it should, at these prices. But I am celebrating. I am not fussing about money, of which I have plenty. It's almost seven and I haven't eaten. I order room service: green chile pork loin, roasted squash, biscochitos, and mango sorbet for dessert (two scoops).

While I wait for the food to arrive, I hang up my dress and change into lounging pajamas and a robe, compliments of the house. I'm scrolling through email—Max's, not mine—when the first text arrives.

"I'm ready to go."

I ignore the message. Max is not a man of patience. Within four minutes the second text arrives.

"Where are you? I'm ready."

This time I reply. "I don't give a shit." I take several seconds to savor the look I know is on my husband's face. There might even be a slight chest pain, which adds to my short-lived savoring.

"WTF is going on Toni?"

"Whatever the fuck I want."

"What are you talking about?"

I can feel Max's anger and his confusion embedded in those five words.

"I'm done."

"What do you mean done?"

"What word is confusing you?"

Room service arrives. I shut my phone off for the night.

The presentation goes well. The Altuzarra was absolutely the right choice. The VP of Commercial Banking asks for a copy of my PPT, and I overhear the chief banking officer saying they were impressed. I smooth the front of my dress and head down to the lobby. That's where our main branch is located, and it's where I get a money order using funds Max doesn't yet know he donated to our joint account. The money order doesn't last long. I walk across the street to one of the big four branches, but not the biggest, and open an account. I deposit my new funds into my latest new account.

I treat myself to some soy latte macchiato espresso thing that costs eight dollars. It's outrageous, but I have found money. I smile and smooth the front of my dress.

I need to talk to Alex, my boss. He's fair and approachable and open to ideas. I want a few days off. I have the time, and Alex will not pry why the sudden request. I'm wondering though how much

I should share. We have worked together for five years; we are both part of the leadership team. We're adults.

In my mental list of Alex's attributes, I forgot "astute." The request has barely left my lips when my boss asks, casually and without probing or judgment, "Everything okay?"

I decide to dive in, perhaps a result of the eight-dollar macchiato. "I'm leaving Max. I need a few days to get organized."

Alex nods. He's divorced, twice. "Where are you staying?"

It doesn't occur to me that Alex would invite me to stay with him. It doesn't occur to Alex either. "The corporate casita near Gateway Park has just been renovated. It's vacant. Will likely stay vacant for some time. It's yours if you'd like."

I would indeed like.

The bank condo is the corporate equivalent of the Courtyard: moderately posh. Three walls of windows let light flood the main room and the three bedrooms. The light bounces off the turquoise pillows, turquoise mat threads, turquoise picture frames. There are vases and coasters and plants, just like someone actually lives here. And now someone does.

It's not home, but it wouldn't take much. A few photos, perhaps of my trip to Taos, and something uniquely me. A mirror, maybe? Magazines?

My first night in my new home goes well. Omelet for dinner. Expensive Scotch for dessert. I forego TV and opt for a deep dive into Max's online presence. Doesn't look like he's tried to access his bank account. It will take some time to get into that since I changed the password. His HR rep sent an email to say that his paycheck will now be deposited directly in the joint account. I reply, and I savor my Scotch.

Tuesday is busy. I spend some time finding a small trucking company that can help me move my clothes and a few possessions out of the house on Thursday, when Max is at his conference. I am always surprised at what people charge for the most basic of services. I also make an appointment with a divorce lawyer. I want to know my rights, and a separation agreement sounds prudent. Investment bankers are prudent at heart.

Max has not texted me since Sunday, so he is staying true to form. This is swagger. He will show me. He will not come crawling. He will not bend. I am indifferent.

On Wednesday I visit the three liquor stores closest to me and stock up on boxes for the move tomorrow. I also stop by the dry cleaner to get my remaining clothes. I have another coupon. Brevity sighs. I take another look at the disaster area that is her office. I share her disapproval.

I am amazed that the condo is beginning to feel like home, to feel like mine. I remind myself that it is not mine; it is the bank's property. Then again, I work for the bank. Dinner is salmon and more expensive Scotch for dessert. Tomorrow is moving day.

It goes without a hitch. I check Find My Friends. (Max is on my list; I am not on his.) The blue dot assures me that he is on the plane as I am making my way to the old house. Only one trip is required to load up the truck. By noon my clothes are unpacked, my jewelry sorted, and my shoes lined up by season in the walk-in closet. I'm finished.

I don't feel finished.

My sister-in-law texts me mid-afternoon and asks if I'm free for dinner. The message jolts me. I've been so focused on rearranging my life, right down to pictures from my winter vacation, that I had not thought about the implications of that rearrangement on people I care about. My sister-in-law is one of those. (My mother-in-law is not.)

I text Rhoda back to apologize, say I'm working late, and ask for a raincheck. It will not be the meal she expects. There is no way Max will have told his family what's going on; admitting things are not perfect in his world is not his style. Rhoda will not be surprised, I think, but she will be disappointed. I schedule a recurring date in my calendar: Call Rhoda.

Rhoda's message has, ironically perhaps, quelled my discomfort. I understand now that I was in limbo. Not a place I like to be. But I'm no longer in limbo. I'm done.

Well, almost done.

I get in the car and drive across town to the dry cleaner. I make my way past the crisis zone and walk to the front counter. Brevity doesn't bother to smile.

"More clothes?" She waves to the racks of plastic outfits swaying behind her.

"I'm not here for clothes. I want the mannequin." I point to the cotton dress form hanging precariously from a stainless-steel rack lying in three pieces on the dusty floor.

Now I have Brevity's attention. She likely thinks I've been drinking. She probably also thinks she can take advantage of me. She's wrong on both counts.

"Fifty dollars."

It's a ridiculous price. We both know it. We settle on twenty. Brevity goes to get the mannequin from behind the barricade. She plops it in front of the door and returns to the cash register. I slide a coupon across the counter.

The mannequin is standing stage left in my living room. It's wearing the cream-colored presentation dress. Lovely.

I sit with the last of my Scotch and stare at the mannequin. I should be savoring, but something is missing. It takes me three sips. I head for my bedroom and the jewelry armoire.

There it is, the boho necklace I purchased in Taos. The large turquoise stones set off the dress perfectly and complement the condo's décor. A designer couldn't have planned it better.

I put my feet up on the couch and grin. I like it when things work out as they should. My only regret: I will need to find a closer dry cleaner.

And I hope they take coupons.

donalee Moulton's poetry and short stories have appeared in literary journals across Canada and the U.S. including Prairie Fire, The Dalhousie Review, The Antigonish Review, *and* Carousel. *She is a former editor of* The Pottersfield Portfolio *literary journal. An original version of "Mannequin" was published in* Queen's Quarterly.

I SMASH MY SKULL AGAINST THE AMERICAN DREAM

Kirbie Bennett

& then the alarm clock screams against the morning sun. the alarm clock wakes me up & reminds me that everyone I love will one day bring me sorrowroses. what I'm saying is we are somewhere south of peace drenched in hell-soaked earth & during the weekdays I'm resuscitating an anemic will to live & I'm indecisive over what to eat because I can't find justice in a grocery store where on the corner of 9th & Camino, an old woman looks at all the vehicles roaring with oblivion & the woman folds her arms, waiting for the world to obey her & in my aunt's house she tapes to the walls obituaries of family, they look like roots reaching for a tree: then she says *heaven is a verb* & fate spells it like that one afternoon in Buckley Park, surrounded by emergency heartbeats, you're standing beside me, we are marching through the downtown streets because this country loves its sins dressed in chains & uranium, so we are shouting rage over wars that never end, we are planting seeds with aching tears & when the rally is over you take one more look at this gathering, you smile at everyone before leaving & the next day you're gone from the living world & now I keep asking:

who put this heart in my chest? I never got a chance to thank them because god has a habit of reaching out & ripping away the people I love & then I'm left with traffic lights & time clocks pulling at my teeth. I mean, I spend lunch breaks finding new rooms to explore in my skull's architecture of grief & at night I can feel sadness growing deeper in the foundation, decorated around every doorway & in this structure there are no windows but I invent them. & in my dreams I keep returning to this vision: it's a night on earth & we're in that home with a candle always burning & together we're removing all our daily defeats, we're spreading records out across the floor, we leave the music on, we collect all the clocks & toss time into a fire: we never leave the room & for a flickering moment no one dies

Kirbie Bennett is an essayist, poet, and audio producer. His work has appeared in various publications, including High Country News, *KSUT* Public Radio, *and* Chapter House Journal. *He is also part of the creative team behind* The Magic City of the Southwest, *a regional history podcast. Kirbie is from the Navajo Nation, and Durango is another place he calls home.*

Foreshadowing

Mimi Gorman

April 17, 2025

For 20 miles, the speed limit is mostly 35 mph, sometimes 45. Today, I cannot sustain even 25. I unwittingly decelerate multiple times to appreciate the prehistoric timeline exposed and contoured by erosion. A landscape that has welcomed people to inhabit its hallows and cuestas for millennia. A terrain which is wild and vulnerable, scarred by fire yet alive with regrowth.

Beside the rim of successive, shallow canyons, the two-way, paved road which I am traveling undulates and bends frequently like a game trail. Today, I am grateful for how the land and road are woven together, and the lack of linear lengths of pavement. There is no time to speed, or time to worry about the future as I monitor my peripheral surroundings and my jaw slips into awe.

The analogy of powdered sugar sifted atop a chocolate pastry is trite, yet it arouses several senses. It also interprets my experience this morning driving the park road. It is mid-April. A light, crepuscular snowfall highlights the gradual slopes forming canyon walls. Meadows are marbled with whiteness where the snow fell and perhaps melted a bit, creating a mosaic of white on dark. Snow persists on the brittle gray-brown branches of trees burned years ago and is affixed to the crooked lines of dormant shrubs. I have seen this before but never have I been so aroused by the collective beauty depicting a farewell to winter.

Navigating the curve that bends like a gibbous moon around Park Point, the highest elevation within Mesa Verde National Park, I have had enough. I can no longer safely drive through a scenery that is distracting me. Oncoming traffic is null. I drive across the left lane and swerve to a stop in a pullout. A cloud formation in the distant atmosphere renders me spellbound.

About 17 miles away in the western sky is Southwest Colorado's tallest landmark, Ute Mountain, respectfully known to many as Sleeping Ute. Beneath the 9984 feet (3043 m) summit, water vapor has condensed into an elongated, swollen, puffy mass. It dawdles as if in a sustained embrace with the mountain.

I step outside the warmth of my forest-green Outback, embracing the cold. Sunlight is muted. The sky, particularly to my left whence I came, is a guise of inconsistently layered dusky blue and subtle gray hues. A silence, sans a few passing cars—co-workers, no doubt— surrounds me as it engulfs the shallow canyon and climbs to the highest peak. My mind's eye watches it gently rebound between the canyon walls, contra to the forceful bellow of wind which regularly stakes claim here. While my mind falls prey to the silence, my body unconsciously adopts a meditation.

I typically drive this road between 7 and 8 a.m. It never fails that I am surprised by an animal—coyote, bear, bobcat, hawk, raven—or sunlight shifting with the hour and season. Even the changing busyness along the road warrants alertness. But the natural tranquility, simplicity and painterliness observed in this moment leads me to proclaim it the most captivating morning I have witnessed at this national park.

This peaceful reprieve from the unconscionable drama unfolding in America and the uncertainty of my own status as a civil servant is short-lived. A shiver alerts me and my whole self regains consciousness.

I return to the heated seat of my car. The speakers return my mind to the audio book, which picks up where it was interrupted by my exit. Shockingly, I realize that the title of the audio book, which I had randomly selected from the shelves of Mancos Public Library, offers an eerie sentiment on the state of the union or perhaps even a personal portend.

I Hate to Leave this Beautiful Place is a memoir by Howard Norman. The title crushes my soul as I watch the snow gradually disappear and the cloud hugging Ute Mountain redesigning its surface. Along the remaining ten miles of my drive, I consider the unwelcomed possibility of waving good-bye to this beautiful place.

The administration of the United States has created social, economic, and environmental uncertainties. People, real people like my National Park Service community, are witnessing the erasure of jobs and protective regulations for public land, and our personal liberties risk expungement.

It isn't just my job that has me concerned. It is the welfare of this beautiful place, the people who nurture it, and those who come to experience it.

Monday, May 5, 2025

I am listening to the final pages of the audio book, *I Don't Want to Leave This Beautiful Place*. Before entering the tunnel, which connects two canyons along Park Road, I return to chapter 15. The author recalls a favorite quote by Robert Frost, "The best way out is always through."

As I go through the tunnel, I ponder how those words apply to my life. Am I hoping for easy answers? Do I want closure? What am I really going through right now? As I exit the tunnel, discontent and confusion are stationary in the sky and my soul. A gray dullness hangs stagnantly near and far. The peaks of the eastern La Plata Mountains are burdened with clouds.

And as I'm rounding Park Point, Ute Mountain suffocates under a dense shroud. I cannot see through it. I can only assume that Ute Mountain remains a citadel on the horizon.

As I did last month, I cross the left lane and pull to a stop. I gently close the car door as I step out. The wind is bitterly cold and whips through the layers of clothing meant to keep me warm. I search the landscape but there is nothing to hold my attention except for the wind, so I retreat. The bitterness is a portend.

Although I remain in service to Mesa Verde National Park, I was stripped of the privilege to drive this road as a National Park Service employee. The letters NPS have been replaced by DOI, Department of Interior, signifying my new employer. While I remain tethered to these beautiful cuestas and my dedicated co-workers, there is no official clarity to which mission I serve. My heart is attached as it has been since 2005, to "preserve unimpaired the natural and cultural resources and values of the national park system for the enjoyment, education, and inspiration of this and future generations." I choose that as opposed to the underlying mission and current actions of DOI supporting energy, revenue, and policing.

I was not consulted, interviewed, or given notice of the change in my status. Sans an email late Friday afternoon announcing this unsolicited conversion scheduled for Sunday, I would not have known until my arrival at the office today. I was consolidated along with 1,000-plus NPS staff from human resources, IT, and communications. Among these are 229 colleagues who were hired as Visual Information Specialists. We represent a score of different skills and talents, including website content management, social media, film-making, publication creation, exhibit development, and graphic design. But we were singled out as public communicators and therefore lumped under the directive of DOI.

I, with overwhelming solidarity, chose a career with NPS because of its mission, the values, the places, the people, the opportunities, and, yes, even the ubiquitous payment in sunsets for which the NPS is known. The latter, along with sunrises, blossoms, animal tracks, stories, pottery sherds, and the inexhaustible list of undocumented compensation has defined and driven my relationship with Mesa Verde, its neighbors, and ancestral spirits.

Today I stand only for a few seconds outside of my car. The dry, blustery, gloom lingering in the valley and along its slopes has a stronghold within me. The invisibility of Ute Mountain defines the path ahead for me and reflects professional uncertainties. Momentum and passion await revelation.

Tuesday, June 17

A tensile band of dust suspended and compressed simultaneously disconnects Ute Mountain. Visually spits it in two. How many particles are suspended to create such a form extending from the western horizon to the southern reach of my eyes? A light blue sky forms the backdrop to the contrasting sepia tone of the obtrusive, linear demarcation. It startles me.

I decelerate around the bend at Park Point, but today I do not stop. The unpredictability and confusion surrounding my job prevails. However, I allow Ute Mountain, both the summit protruding above the dust band, and its stout body below, to inform me. I hear a message to hang in there. Go through it. Be steady. Everything eventually comes together.

Yesterday, 74 staff from the colleagues who were unsuspectedly consolidated into the authority of the Department of Interior were restored to work directly for NPS. I was not one of them. I celebrate their return to the green-and-gray uniform! Meanwhile, I continue shifting through phases of grief highlighted by anger and submission into some form of acceptance, just to get by while I wait for whatever decisions follow.

Since 2003, when I responded to a call for volunteers at the Hoh Rainforest in Olympic National Park, and since accepting my first seasonal offer at Mount Rainier National Park in 2005, I have donned an NPS uniform including the iconic flat hat and badge. I joyfully wept with pride the first day I wore the full NPS official regalia. Even though I have not worn the uniform much in the past 18 months due to my office responsibilities, it remains a steady reminder of my commitment and passion, and it is a stronghold of the oath which I signed, to uphold the Constitution of the United States of America.

Five days a week Ute Mountain comes into my view and harkens me to slow. Most days, as I take air and earth for granted, it passes my vision without acknowledgement. Regional mountain ranges such as the La Platas and San Juans claim more presence and notability. Regardless, Ute Mountain stands as a monument to the past and a guidepost for now and hereafter. As a silhouette in the dust or a beacon in the sun, to witness and be mentored by Ute Mountain fills me with gratitude.

Like all civil servants, I do not know when the axe might fall, or when public lands will lose their designation, or when protection and preservation will cease for national parks. At least for now I have a job, within a beautiful place. A place that holds millennia of living truths and molds the truth within me. A place, even in the heart of summer, that curtsies as I pass along the road.

Mimi Gorman has been with the National Park Service as a full-time visual information specialist, seasonal interpretive park ranger, and volunteer since 2003. Her writing journey continues to fulfill a childhood dream to share outside experiences through words.

I Looked For Lilacs Everywere We Went

Beth Buczynski

First, in the spring,
outside the window of the bedroom we shared
in the apartment I didn't realize was for poor people.

(I sometimes wonder who planted them there,
in the corners where somber brick buildings met
— who gave us amethysts for free?)

Then, in the South,
a talisman of home, the clustered familiar.
Forcing a rare smile across our father's tired face

— the most beautiful scent in the world, he'd say.

Then, as we wound our way across the Rockies,
I learned why they're often found in rows,
along a fence line or behind an aging farmhouse.

"...to mark a miscarriage"
and, "outhouses."

life and death and shit and flowers

— always all at once,
and parading just outside the window.

Beth Buczynski has rambled all over, but the mountains have always been home. In 2023, she and her husband settled in La Plata County, where the San Juans are teaching them stillness and a bit of self-sufficiency. A version of this poem was published previously on the author's Medium profile.

Traces of the SaltWitch

H.C. Petley

When SaltWitch first came into the country, the people didn't know her. She came to them as a young woman no one had ever seen before. The land was different then. Many lakes and streams were fed by springs of sweet water. Many kinds of plants and animals we don't see anymore filled the valleys and roamed the hills.

The Blue Cloud people of the south were the first to perceive the true intentions of SaltWitch. She was known as Salt Woman then. She never seemed to grow old. The people began to suspect she was a witch and they were afraid of her. Kontochi'i, the guardian snake of the south, warned the people not to partake of her pasu, a salt-water elixir that she offered them. When the people refused her, she began to change the land with great fires. She dried up the springs of sweet water. She chased many of the animals away. Kontochi'i warned the people not to forget their songs lest they become p'waquas, slaves to Salt Woman, witches who use up the string of life.

SaltWitch is one of the sisters of Sun Father Yat'Kai T'Accu. Her name in the ancient tonguewas Malokatsiki. She turned to evil ways due to jealousy. Long ago she was spurned by RainMaster, Ta'Tahokohika. The Corn Maidens were favored by RainMaster and that is why SaltWitch began to hate them. She began to work against the people who worshiped the Corn Maidens. She cast many spells and sought to dry up the land, strangle the springs of sweet water, turn lakes into dust of alkali.

The Corn Maidens are seven in number and of seven colors: blue, yellow, white, red, black, speckled, and green for when the corn is young. The people of the many villages made songs and ceremonies to honor the Corn Maidens, for they were beautiful and radiant under a blessing from Sun Father, and gifts of the Storm Kings. The villagers worshiped their beauty and their sweetness. SaltWitch hated them because of their sweetness and their beauty and because of the devotion showed to them by the people of the land.

SaltWitch is the enemy of the Masked Gods, who are the Storm Kings of the West. They are the sons of RainMaster, regulators of the clouds bringing rain and snow to the land and to the people of the land. The Corn Maidens are beholden to the Storm Kings and worship them with many songs of thankfulness and respect. Without the favor of the Storm Kings, rain and snow would not fall. Corn would not grow tall. For this reason, because she is jealous of the Corn Maidens, SaltWitch is the enemy of those Masked Gods. She is always fighting with them.

In the ancient days the people learned to make bricks from mud and sagebrush. They became skilled at weaving baskets from grass and other plant fibers. They grew cotton, maize, beans, squash, and pumpkins, and kept flocks of turkeys for meat and eggs. Many years went by, many times the life of one person. SaltWitch was rarely seen. For a time she was not seen at all. It was said she was sleeping. And yet the land continued to dry up. The vegetation changed.

Even though sleeping, her spells were still at work. While SaltWitch slept, the people forgot about her. The powers of the Corn Maidens grew strong. Songs and ceremonies were composed to honor them. The people prospered.

The Red Cloud people of the West were the first to know that SaltWitch had awakened. When she stretched and yawned there was a great shaking of the land. Many houses collapsed and the people were afraid. Some small streams ceased to flow. Springs dried up. SaltWitch was slow to awaken. The land was quiet for many years thereafter.

SaltWitch created the Dark Horns at the end of the day, at the time right before the sun pulls down all the light. Dark Horn people were of many tribes, different clans, different cultures. They were people who wanted power, wanted to be p'waquas, sorcerers who gained great strength and ability of mind and body. SaltWitch gave them her pasu, her saltwater elixir, and began to teach them her spells of longevity, of dominance by force of will, of waiting. She began to send her Dark Horns into the villages to turn the people against the Corn Maidens.

The Dark Horns were few at first. They came at the edge of night, sundown figures moving in from the shadows of the rangeland. At first the people paid them little attention. They appeared to be very old, with skin dry like an old snake, wanderers seeking water, but never asking for food. They began to use the spells taught to them by SaltWitch. The people barely noticed the drying of the land, and didn't learn the ways of the Dark Horns.

SaltWitch summoned her favored Dark Horns in the twilight when the first sliver of moon appeared in the sky. These five she made chieftains and gave them jish, gave them powers over time and space. The five had already attained the power of force of will and had the ability to coerce others to obey their commands. They began to attract followers, finding them on the outskirts of villages, those who had been scorned or driven out, those who welcomed the Dark Horns and wanted to be like them. Over time, the chieftains formed bands of slave traders who preyed upon villages along the Rio, especially those that worshiped the Corn Maidens.

In time the people began to forget their songs to the Corn Maidens. They neglected their rituals and their ceremonies. Ceremony keeps people thinking in proper ways, keeps people together. The Dark Horns infected the ceremonies with confusion. People began to quarrel and practice the witchcraft of the Dark Horns, using spells against one another. They began to keep after material things, desired to grow rich, desired to dominate others and keep them as slaves. Gossip ruled villages and people forgot to help one another on the path of life.

During this time the p'waquas of the Dark Horn, empowered by SaltWitch, attempted to capture the Corn Maidens. These p'waquas wanted to enslave all the magic of the Corn Maidens and all the people who worshiped them. The spells woven to entrap the Corn Maidens were very strong and caused them to flee for safety. In the village of the Masked Gods, far beyond the rim of the West, they found sanctuary. Chohakwa'i, chief of the Storm Kings, took them in and protected them. He gave them a sacred lake, and they made a place to live hidden along its shores. The Dark Horns of SaltWitch could not find them.

For the lives of many people, new generations replacing old, SaltWitch was seen or not seen. She was the talk of many legends and stories. Many times her hand was felt guiding her Dark Horns. Some say she would appear as a beautiful woman, alluring to men with her whispers and promises. Others say she was a wicked hag who lived in a cave at the end of a box canyon.

Once SaltWitch came to a certain village. That village did not worship the Corn Maidens, nor did they pay tribute to the Dark Horns. She came at the end of the day, an old woman in ragged clothes begging food and water. The people of that village were proud and fierce. They did not recognize her, and they refused her, driving her out of their village.

SaltWitch called her grandson, Rock Lizard Boy. One morning he led the children out of the village to play. The old woman gathered them all together and bewitched them, turning them into jay birds and scattering them into the piñon trees.

In those days, the most powerful of the Dark Horn p'waquas inhabited an old pueblo long abandoned by its builders. SaltWitch had driven those people out, brought great suffering upon them because they continued to worship the Corn Maidens. They failed to pay tribute to SaltWitch. She caused their springs to dry up in a great shaking of the land. Without fresh water, crops failed. She caused their sons and daughters to weaken and die from a strange illness. Those people decided they would have to move away, leaving the pueblo empty. Many years passed, and during that time the Dark Horns moved in. That pueblo became one of their strongholds.

Without the power of the Corn Maidens, without the favor of the Storm Kings, the people began to suffer. The land was changed greatly. Whole lakes of sweet water dried up and evaporated into pans of alkali. Streams ceased to flow. Many of the great animals were taken away into the spirit realm where they dwell to this day. Hot winds scoured the hills, and the air was filled with blowing sand. Corn did not grow tall, and the people knew hunger. Springs ceased to bubble, and the people knew thirst. Dark Horns ruled many villages. Memory of the Corn Maidens faded like dreams from long ago.

In a certain village, only one family kept the ways of the Corn Maidens. The name of that village is forgotten in time. This family was a mother, a father, three daughters, and their husbands. They did not follow the ways of the Dark Horns. They began to teach a group of boys the ceremonies of corn and showed them the places where the Storm Kings, the most powerful of the Masked Gods, made rain. These boys became strong and learned in the ways of plants and the songs of healing. The people began calling them the Medicine Flower Boys.

The Medicine Flower Boys were seven in number. In time they learned to make the prayer sticks necessary to please the Corn Maidens. They learned these ways so they could ask them to return to the people and give their blessings once again. The Medicine Flower Boys resisted the spells of SaltWitch and her Dark Horn p'waquas. After many years of serving the people and many tests of their sincerity, their songs and prayers to the Corn Maidens were received.

Over the many years that the Medicine Flower Boys learned and practiced the ways of the Corn Maidens they had many challenges from SaltWitch and her followers. In time, these disciples of the Medicine Flower Way grew to young manhood. They followed the paths of the warriors of their people.

The most powerful of the Dark Horn p'waquas forced many peaceful villages to pay them tribute. These Dark Horns knew the ways of SaltWitch, of longevity, of waiting, of subjugation by force of will. They kept many slaves and traded them to others. Under the spells of the Dark Horns, slave traders took root in that old pueblo and held it for many years. They worshiped SaltWitch and paid her p'waquas tribute of slaves. They wanted to obtain the spells of longevity and of domination. For many terrible years, these slavers raided gardens and settlements and pueblos of various tribes who lived along the Great River. Water flowed there and the magic of the Corn Maidens was still strong in those places.

A delegation of elders went to meet with the devotees of the Medicine Flower Way and asked them to help against the Dark Horn slave traders. Even though their warriors were now strong young men, wise beyond their years and skilled in the ways of the world, the people still called them the Medicine Flower Boys.

The Medicine Flower Boys went down into their kiva, which was in a secret place hidden far from the knowledge of SaltWitch. They held ceremony there that lasted three days. All that took place during that ceremony is not known, for no one today has been told those secrets. A vow was made to destroy the slave traders and the Dark Horn p'waquas who gave them power.

The battle began in the dark of night, when the moon was gone from the sky. For three nights and three days unceasing the conflict raged until, at last, all the slave traders were killed. Many young people and children were set free. The Dark Horn witches were subdued and their spells broken. Many of them were swallowed by the earth and others simply turned to salt and crumbled.

At the end of the third day, a great cloud of rain billowed out of the west and a double rainbow appeared. A messenger came from beyond the clouds and the Medicine Flower Warriors were shown the path that leads to the village of the Masked Gods. No other mortals have ever been permitted to enter this village. Their songs and prayers to the Corn Maidens and to the Storm Kings were given great favor.

The Corn Maidens returned to the people. They taught anew the ways of virtue and the songs of plenty. The Storm Kings brought rain and washed the dry land, cleansing the countryside of salt and alkali. Chohakwai'i subdued SaltWitch and broke many of her spells. He confined her to the barren lands of the far south.

SaltWitch was forbidden to take away any more sweet water and forbidden to go to the tops of the mountains where snow and ice gather to refresh the land. She was given a cave to live in under a dry lakebed, and there she remains to this day.

Traces of SaltWitch can be found by those who care to search beyond the edges of highways. Her spells of drying and of waiting are at work. Her hand moves the plans of her Dark Horns. Her whispers can be heard in the hot, dry winds that blow across the shifting sands and etch the ragged corners of the canyons.

Now 84, H. C. Petley began his checkered writing career in 1960 at the University of Pittsburgh. His byline has been posted in such disparate places as the Mainichi News, Astrophysics Newsletter, Galaxy Magazine, Los Angeles Free Press, *Playboy's* OUI Magazine, *and many others now out of print and forgotten. His picaresque comedy novel* Queen of Slots *was selected by the Merchant Marine Library of NYC for distribution to all the ships at sea during the Gulf War. Rare copies can sometimes be found at Amazon's Abe Books. Currently, he lives quietly in Cortez.*

Vernal Equinox

Edward A. Stabler

We cross the sodden chalk
and sad grass of an empty playing field,
damp and drained of color,
like the pale grass now in that fading snapshot,
when you kicked a ball with your hair and forearms shining
during an hour of fifth-grade recess in the sun.

And from this hash-mark, at 44 –
or now this one, or the next – when you squint
you can see the glimmering arcs of time to both horizons,
their lengths and promises balanced,
the illusion of a chosen arc fragile but intact,
like melting sculpted ice.

But the waters of those past springs recede,
and underfoot today faint currents rise

to course, unbidden, toward another spring.
Awake, asleep, alone, together –
they sweep us forward in their careless arms.

Edward A. Stabler moved to Durango from the Washington, DC area in 2017. Links to his six e-novels are available at https://khola.com.

Storm-chasing on the Lower Dolores, a National Conservation Priority

Or how your hero found himself pursued by search-and-rescue professionals and sheriff's deputies from three counties in the remote canyons of a proposed national conservation area

Matt Barnes

O
ne October in the red-rock country, I saw that flash flooding on the northwest side of the San Juan Mountains had brought the rarely-boatable lower Dolores River from a rusty trickle to a few thousand cubic feet per second—*The lower Dolores is flashing—load up the kayak!* I'd been "working" on this personal project for years because McPhee Dam very nearly stops the river's flow; boatable releases don't even happen in most years, and when they do, they're over quickly. This flood would unleash a chain of events involving search-and-rescue and law enforcement professionals from three counties—but first, I should explain a little about the remote and spectacular Dolores River canyon country.

The Dolores is a personal paddling priority, and a national conservation priority. For decades, conservationists, agencies, landowners, and representatives have collaborated to protect the Dolores River canyons below McPhee Dam. It is the largest, most biodiverse area of unprotected public land in Colorado. The bipartisan Dolores River National Conservation Area and Special Management Area Act, introduced by Colorado Senators Michael Bennet and John Hickenlooper, is a compromise that would protect the river from McPhee Dam through Montezuma, Dolores, and San Miguel counties—and almost everyone involved agrees that it's a step in the right direction, though it does not include the entire landscape worthy of protection. It leaves out the rest of the river corridor to the north, through Montrose and Mesa counties, which could be protected by the proposed Dolores Canyons National Monument, or perhaps another national conservation area. The latter would be preferable, in my opinion, because it would probably better maintain the remote character and low visitor use. Both proposals would allow all current land uses but prevent new ones. Neither proposal would put water back in the river, but both would promote watershed resilience, and protect against future water development.

So that night, boat loaded, I called my Leading Lady, who was out of town, actually working. *If there is still enough water in the morning, I am going to paddle the lower Dolores, where there is no cell signal, and won't be back right away.* Apparently, I didn't emphasize the uncertainty of my return timing. As they say, "the worst problem with communication is the illusion that it happened."

The first day, I scouted a few access points and settled on the last section of the Dolores I hadn't yet paddled, in the northern half, with its controversial proposed designations. I dragged my kayak across untracked mud—*no one else is here, my escape from civilization is complete!*—and paddled the half-melted chocolate milkshake through Paradox Canyon, and down past the San Miguel River, which more than doubled the river's flow. That night I camped between a sandstone arch with a trickle of water flowing through it, and the historic hanging flume—*a symbol of man's folly if I ever saw one, but pretty cool nonetheless.*

The second day, I was paddling blissfully down the canyon,

when a small yellow plane rudely interrupted my solitude, circling several times before buzzing low over me. I recognized it as belonging to a fellow search-and-rescue volunteer from Montezuma County, and waved—using all five fingers.

Mid-afternoon, as I was halfway through the proposed national monument, a white helicopter emblazoned with a seven-pointed sheriff's star buzzed over—*something must be going on, is someone lost out here? A manhunt?*—and then descended towards the nearby road. I eddied out, camera ready.

There were voices in the willows and tamarisk on the opposite bank. The brush parted and two sheriff's deputies wearing the uniforms of San Miguel and Montrose counties emerged. "Are you Matt?"

While I was having a grand time, that Certain Special Someone had gone into full-on panic when I didn't call or come home. She called a few of my paddling friends, including a fellow search-and-rescue volunteer, to see if any were on a river adventure with me. And then she called out the troops.

Feeling like a fugitive, embarrassed at being caught—*is there anything illegal about paddling a flood?*—I ferried across the opaque river. The deputies, polite yet stern, explained the situation. The bank was steep and slippery—*they won't try to climb down this to get me, or they'll end up in the river.* Apparently they decided that a mud-covered kayaker wasn't worth any more trouble. *They look pretty disgusted with me, and surely wouldn't allow me to muck up their helicopter...* But I hoped they enjoyed flying their toys around the canyons as much as I enjoyed paddling. I smiled—after they left—when I thought of how the renegade heroes of *The Monkey Wrench Gang* were chased through the canyon country by search-and-rescue.

Several hours and many miles later, with the water dropping and night settling in, I completed my mission, having paddled most of what was then the proposed monument. There was no one else on the river. The next morning, I hitchhiked back the 50-some miles. Incidentally, it was the anniversary of the historic 1911 flood, when monsoon storms inundated towns, washed out bridges along the Dolores and other rivers in southwestern Colorado, and eliminated what little communication there was in much of the Four Corners.

And that smart, lovely, and hopefully forgiving Leading Lady still doesn't remember our conversation the same way I do. No congratulations for finally finishing the last leg of the Dolores that I hadn't paddled before. No awe at the miles I'd paddled. No cheerleader this time.

I'm all for solo backcountry adventures, preferably without deadlines or communications. What is the West if not a place to disappear for a while? But I should know better. Next time I'll write something down, with some explanation about storm-chasing kayakers not having solid itineraries.

More importantly, my hard-earned efforts solidified my opinion that the entire river corridor and surrounding public lands need to be protected. The Dolores River National Conservation Area, as proposed in the southern portion of the watershed, is a middle ground reached through years of negotiation, retains important components of Wild and Scenic suitability, ensures no more dams will be built, and protects existing uses: it will protect the Dolores, but not completely. Complementary proposals for the northern portion of the watershed have been offered. Regardless of the designation—national conservation area, national monument, or both—many Coloradans and river users agree: the time has come to permanently protect this magnificent landscape.

After all, it is the kind of place where cowboys and kayakers could outrun the law, if only the law didn't have a helicopter.

Matt Barnes, a rangeland conservationist, former ranch manager in Montrose County, so-called dirtbag kayaker, and swiftwater rescue vol-

unteer, lives in Dolores, and would make a dashing outlaw with a suitable canyon hideout. He also serves on the board of Dolores River Boating Advocates, a conservation group with a river-running habit. As of 2025, parts of the southern and northern sections of the Dolores canyon country have been proposed as national conservation areas.

Ode to a Dead Poet

Kathleen Holmes

The obituary said you died of

light

    verse.

Ashes from your poems

    will be tossed

    into the wind at

    Two—

followed by a gathering

    on the sidewalk

    to nowhere.

    —there will be food

Having grown up in New Mexico and spent the past thirty-five years in the Four Corners area, Kathleen Holmes draws inspiration from its diverse landscapes and rich history. "Ode to a Dead Poet" was previously published in the SouthWest Writers 2022 anthology, A Diversity of Expression.

Ralph Goes to Hell

Kevin T. Jones

Ralph Carter was struck dead as a dirtclod at 2:12 in the afternoon as he opened a Kinky Friedman novel to spend a few pleasant minutes reading in the folding lounge chair on the concrete slab patio behind his two-story mobile home. He began to wonder if something was wrong when he looked down and saw a vulture pecking at his feet.

"Shoo, shoo," he shouted, but no sound came from his mouth. He tried to kick at the vulture, which was now joined by several crows, a magpie, and two additional vultures, but his legs wouldn't move. He felt like he was sinking through the bottom of his chair. Ralph looked up through the ground and through the lounge chair and saw the vultures pecking away at his body.

Ralph began to suspect that he'd died and gone straight to hell when he suddenly found himself dressed in a pink bathrobe and puffy slippers in an infinitely large retail store standing in one of an infinite number of infinitely long checkout lines holding a plastic shopping basket filled with polyester slacks, disposable diapers, and liter bottles of diet cola. Neil Diamond's "Sweet Caroline" blared over crackling loudspeakers.

After an eternity or two he leaned over to a man standing next to him and asked, "Do these lines ever move?"

"Get a life, peckerhead," the man snapped back. "Where the hell do you think you are, anyway?"

Ralph stepped back, somewhat shocked, and wondered where, indeed, he was. He thought the grouch looked a lot like Richard Nixon. He looked around a little and saw his old neighbor Wick Dillard standing next to Stephen Douglas. And there was Elvis. And Jack Ruby and Francisco Franco and Alfredo Stroessner and Martin Luther King.

What? No, that can't be right. It must be somebody else. Idi Amin, maybe.

Ralph was starting to think that hell wasn't that bad, actually. There was his third-grade teacher, Mrs. Wells. "Good!" he thought, "If anybody deserves hell, she does." Liza Minnelli's "Hello Dolly" blared over crackling loudspeakers.

He saw a few billion other people he didn't know too—even people who must have been there a pretty long time. He saw a beak-nosed fellow dressed in a toga, and a scruffy-looking guy with long hair and a beard that nobody would get close to, and even one guy he was pretty certain must have been an *Australopithecus robustus*. Or at least a *Homo habilis*. In the distance he could see lines of big, hairy people, and others of little people with big heads. Billy Ray Cyrus's "Achy Breaky Heart" blared over crackling loudspeakers.

A twitchy, nervous-acting man came up to him and asked Ralph if he wanted information on buying a timeshare condominium. Ralph shook his head. The man asked again and again, and Ralph kept turning in circles away from him until eventually he was gone. Another man came up to him and stood too close and Ralph could smell beer and fried eggs on his breath, and he told Ralph that he knew the way to salvation, and that believing in the Savior is the only way to keep from going to hell. Ralph replied that they were already in hell, and the man again told him that the only way to keep from going to hell is to believe in the Savior. Ralph pretended to read the label of a diet cola bottle. A large woman with a nose ring and a tattoo of a mouse with big ears on her forearm came up to Ralph and told him that she could cure his back problems with a special massage. Ralph told her he didn't have back problems, and the woman told him that he would, eventually, and that he would be crawling to her on his hands and knees, and it would cost a lot more then. Celine Dion's "Because You Loved Me" blared over crackling loudspeakers.

He was staring at a big, lumpy man, trying to decide if it might be Rodney Dangerfield, when two large and very bald men wearing sleeveless shirts came barging through the lines. Ralph noticed that they both had tattoos all over their arms, and that one of them had bad front teeth.

"Come on, buddy," Bad Teeth growled as he grabbed Ralph's arm. "Corp says to get you out of here." His shopping basket clattered to the floor, and Ralph thirstily watched a cola bottle bounce onto a brown wing-tip shoe.

"Get him the hell out of here," Grouch sneered. "He's a malcontent. A nattering nabob."

"Jesus Christ," Ralph thought. "It is Nixon."

The two bouncers hustled Ralph through the crowd, knocking old ladies and Neanderthals and priests and peasants and presidents and lots of Asians out of the way. They fought their way against a surging stream of souls flowing in through a mile-wide door. "Gettin' a lot more Muslims these days," Bad Teeth remarked. "And hip-hoppers."

When they got to the exit, a single door hidden behind piles of packing crates and pallets, Bad Teeth pulled a fat ring of keys from his pocket and began unlocking the many bolts, padlocks, and bars that secured the door.

"That's probably a code violation," Ralph offered.

Bad Teeth curled his lip as he jerked the last cantankerous lock free. "These don't get much use," he explained as he reached back and took Ralph under the arm. The bouncers swung him back, and then flung him through the open door. "And stay the hell out of here!"

Ralph saw only darkness, and braced himself for a hard landing, which did not come. He felt himself sailing, falling and falling and falling. He closed his eyes tightly and waited, wondering what would come next. He could hear cries and shrieks all around him, and when he heard a particularly loud and hideous wail, surely the cry of a soul tortured beyond belief, he opened his eyes.

Ralph found himself staring straight into the face of Bessie Lee, his one-eyed orange cat. "What the . . .," Ralph exclaimed, sitting up in his lawn chair, still holding Bessie Lee tight against his chest.

There stood his two-story mobile home, right where it always was. Here was Bessie Lee. He wasn't dead anymore.

"Whew," Ralph said to Bessie Lee. "That was freaky."

Kevin T. Jones is an archaeologist and writer. He served seventeen years as State Archaeologist of Utah. His most recent novel is Barbara's Desert Café, *published in 2025. He lives off-grid with his wife Barbara Evert in southwestern Colorado.*

Everything Is a Poem!

Stephanie Moran

After Frank O'Hara's "Today"

A Found Poem

Walking along the strand of the old old ocean
now the San Juan River
stretching from deep umber cliffs to fathomless blue,

I ask:

Who flings a black Zella bra off
to the side of the highway?

Were you deep into a wild ride
in a capacious red pickup truck
and your lover baby could not wait
to touch your naked nipples?

Did you toss your racerback Size L
for freedom,
for the joy of feeling
your flowing twin sisters?

Or did you hurl your annoyance of
Covid weight
that never saw fit
to lose itself?

Were you in Tracy Chapman's fast car
wanting to go
faster still?

Or did you elope with Uncle Frank,
tatted and buzzcutted then,
or Taylor, now braided, unbelted and undone
doing her time in this confined space,
dreary place,
her breasts swelling with baby's milk in a way
that displeased him and his fists.

So take the lively air, Lovely, as Roethke did
and learn by going where you have to go.

Anything can happen here
in these sexy deep as pomegranate
red cliffs
smooth sandstone
sans bra
like your skin, ah! Your smooth cupped babes.

Were you in a fugue state or fever dream
when the Zella no longer fit just right--
one more constriction, one more rule
you couldn't abide and
so, bid it goodbye?

Poetry is worth waking up for
in the abyss of night
as we ponder past The Recapture
and no city lights,
deep time to lift these lines

and consider the power of this black bra
to nurse armies and raise
those girls of many colors
who will solve the mysterious
emperor of all maladies
if we let them live; if we let them live.

Remember: Everything is a poem
and you are here to write it.
Take my pencil. Start with your name, if you like.
There are words enough for all of us.
You come, too.

Leave the Zella where it lies
and imagine with me:

You and your size L breasts
streaming along the strand
flying free from their black confines
pink tips
kissing the open air.

Stephanie Moran lives in the Four Corners of her beloved Colorado. Poetry brought her the love of her life, and it sees her through the best of times and the worst of times.

Home Invasion

Terry Nichols

The walls of my home are alive with invaders. Frisky, brazen, four-legged merrymakers bent on staking claim to my abode.

For years my sturdy walls provided nothing but exceptional insulation, the stacked straw bales rarely attracting displaced creatures. Now and then a mouse squirmed through a crack in the exterior plaster and ventured inside, running across the floor and triggering Coco's deadly claws. Good kitty.

These sporadic visitors kept my aging cat youthful and earning his keep. Until one early summer night, when I awoke to the pitter-patter of dainty feet trotting on the wood-paneled ceiling above my head. There were many feet, many bodies.

I lay in bed with my fur boy, listening to their antics. Swiveling his ears, Coco gazed up, alert mode activated, anticipating combat. A small ball streaked across the loft floor. The crescent-clawed hunter leaped off the bed and pounced, landing with a decisive thud. He whined, craving praise for his mouthful of rodent.

"Good boy," I said. He grinned, flashing his lone canine, and dropped his prey. It scampered over my toes and behind a dresser. Coco stood guard for hours, but the critter had retreated into the walls, foiling the predator. Later I found half a mouse tail on the floor, a dab of blood on its stump.

The trespassers had to go. Although it sounded like a stampeding herd of itty-bitty buffaloes, surely there weren't more than a half-dozen animals. Since the escapee had warned the others about the single-fanged monster, I didn't expect them to expose themselves to easy hunting. I baited live traps with peanut butter on crackers and slipped them through an access door between the ceiling and roof. So began the mouse eradication.

After three nights, the hunt fell into a routine. Just before midnight, the entire gang would run laps on the ceiling planks, leap electrical wires and dance victory jigs. Later, during my deepest REM sleep, one of them entered the trap and sprang the door shut with a clap, awakening me. Frantic thrashing ensued as the mouse tried to escape.

Unable to sleep through the clatter, I moved the trap and prisoner to the holding area outside on the porch. The mob calmed down the rest of the night, and I slept without further disturbance.

Soon after dawn, I walked down the road with the trap, the frightened captive balled up at one end. Beneath the protective branches of a juniper, I raised the release door and coaxed the trembling creature into the wide world. "Good luck at the bottom of the food chain," I called as it dashed to freedom. I always emptied leftover bait, hoping to reduce the mouse's stress from searching for food.

Just a few days—that's all I'd need to capture the entire horde. Or so I thought. A couple of weeks into the hunt, I'd caught a victim nearly every night and they were still coming. An extended family of deer mice had found refuge in the straw bales and was dining on seeds. Unfazed, I continued my operation.

I kept a running count, noting the personality of each detainee. Most were eager to flee from temporary captivity in the trap, but Number 13 tugged at my heart. He stayed inside the receptacle, crumpled and paralyzed, refusing to move when I opened the door.

"Go! Find your peeps, dude. You can do it!" My pep talk failed. When I finally shook him out, he cowered on the ground for the longest time, shocked by the unfamiliar dirt and scrubby plants. The bedraggled creature limped away into a strange new land.

Mouse Number 15 was totally different. While under confinement, he gnawed the plastic nub where the spring door catches to reset the trap, destroying that device for future use. I admired his fighting spirit to do something—anything—to escape.

Then there was Number 25, the victim of a terrifying ordeal. Early in the morning, I put him on the back stoop as usual while I got more snooze time. When I returned, he had disappeared, along with the trap.

My suspicion: a packrat kidnapper. They love collecting things. Hauling a plastic box with a live emotional support animal to his treasure pile would be the heist of the century. I inspected my boneyard, home for many packrats over the years, and my open-air shed, where a packrat had recently collected den materials. No trap. Coyote? Would a coyote nab the container off my doorstep and run for it, thinking he could extract the small mammal for a snack?

I wiped that disturbing thought from my mind and focused. "Don't worry, I'll find you. Squeak loudly, okay?" I circled my house, reassuring my charge as I searched under sage bushes and checked juniper limbs as if a wildcat had dragged him up there. The sun rose higher, and the morning grew warmer. If I didn't spot him within a few hours, that confined animal would roast like a chestnut in an agonizing, cruel death. I had to find him.

After forty-five more minutes of stumbling around, I threw my head back and arms into the air. "I surrender! Oh packrat ruffians, coyote snitches, and mouse guardians, I pray. Please, please, *please* help me find that scared little guy."

There it was. A glint of plastic between the water barrel and the house wall. An upside-down trap and a right-side-up mouse, gnawing his own paws, glassy eyes bulging. His packrat abductor had dragged the contraption over rocks and plants and abandoned his quarry midway on the journey to the shed.

"Poor wittle mousie! I put you in grave danger." I covered my face in shame. "Thank goodness your divine protectors saved you." I left an extra ration of peanut butter for Number 25 when I let him go.

Days passed and my running total mounted. Now when I left the trap on the stoop in the dead of night, I covered it with an overturned bucket to protect it from kidnappers. I switched from peanut butter to tahini on crackers, which seemed to attract even more hungry victims.

During every release I declared, "Last one, *this* is it." But more skitters, slap of the trapdoor, and I had one more. As days went on, my statement turned to a whine. A demand. A plea. They didn't stop coming. Several nights I caught four mice, two before going to bed, and hauled them each to freedom in the moonlight.

Adults and youngsters with ungainly ears, swooping tails, and bodies quivering from racing, supercharged hearts. All had innocent black eyes and pinprick claws, so teeny on those miniature padded tootsies, so perfect for climbing plaster. Under the eaves high above the ground, I stuffed steel wool in cracks where the plaster met the vigas and metal roof. Without a tall ladder, I couldn't reach the spot where a red-shafted flicker had pecked the plaster clean off the bale. The door to my rodent resort was wide open.

Word spread in the neighborhood about the elegant digs and kinky mouse parties going down at my address. No doubt the released mice raced back with buddies in tow, eager to scale the wall and join the rabble-rousers.

As my campaign continued, I slept less and grew more cranky. "Bad Coco! Get into those walls and show them who's boss!" My trophy hunter licked his paws, inured to the constant scrabbles. I dreaded the sound of a trapdoor snapping, detested the nighttime jaunt and bleary-eyed trudge in the wee hours. Vermin invaded my dreams, squeaked and lectured, and overturned my idyllic life.

Mouse Number 64 underscored the enormity of the situation. I caught her one night, too late to venture out to release her. I say "her" because she was big and round and very pregnant. At least I'd caught her before she could drop her young in my walls. I didn't expect the miracle of life to occur by dawn, however. She delivered four nubbin babies outside on my stone porch where she couldn't keep them warm. Her naked newborns expired. In my live trap.

"Oh, sweetie, what have I done? Please forgive me." Sobbing, I released Mama Mouse Number 64 and her dead babes. My heart ached as they tumbled to the cold earth, far from her cozy nest lined with Coco's fur, tucked into my straw bales.

A vow took root in my sagging heart: squelch the pestilence, once and for all. Number 64 confirmed they were reproducing, perpetuating a dynasty that could rule for decades. Research told me deer mice breed any time of year with up to eleven and an average of four to six pups per litter. Females reach sexual maturity after thirty-five days. If I didn't get them all in one growing cycle, they would forever inhabit my realm. I was on the brink of permanent infestation.

More traps, more bait, more captures. I opened a second jar of tahini, desperate to halt the breeding and eradicate them all by winter.

Months into my crusade, after I freed Number 115, it happened. Door sprung, bait gone, no mouse. At the other end of the trap, the release door—manipulated only by human fingers—was raised. Somehow, the varmint maneuvered it to escape.

For several nights they outwitted the traps, stealing the bait without getting caught. The only plausible explanation: they were teaming up. One mouse secured the spring door while her partner snatched the treat. Or else one danced across the trap like a floating ballerina, without triggering the spring mechanism. Sometimes, they sprang the door and left the food. Just to wake me up, provoke my curses, torment me.

Whatever their diabolical schemes, captures eventually stopped and the bait grew stale.

But they're still here.

Sometimes I hear a scamper. Whispers. Plotting.

They've learned. As social animals, they snuggle together and share the legends of gallivanting Grandpa and wandering Whiskers, who indulged their cravings, only to be carried off to distant lands or get pierced by a sharp fang. Now they know to avoid food in the plastic deli. The kingpin issued warnings. "If you want to stay in our comfy haven, forgo the box and shun the butter."

Wiser and more determined than ever, they cavort and titter and weave their plans while churning out offspring to colonize their stronghold in the straw bale walls. The roiling, rumbling walls of my home.

Terry Nichols is a retired National Park Service ranger who worked mostly in the American Southwest. Her middle grade novel, The Dreaded Cliff, *stars a word-mangling, hopelessly lost packrat. She writes from her home in Aztec. A version of this essay appeared September 2022 at her website, https://terryfnichols.com/.*

Our Mayfly Days

Peter Martori

As a young man I learned
about Mayflies. I struggled to make
sense of their brief lives,
compared to the ancient Redwood
trees and mine.

If time was any measure of worth
what is the worth of a Mayfly's life–
or mine– compared to the Redwood's?

A child dies in her crib,
an old man rolls a cigarette
and tells stories of a time
before time began,

what a waste, an overdose

a suicide, a car full of kids
on their last ride, a starlet
cut down in her prime,
a man who had it all
stopped short, before his time.

They say time seems to quicken
the older we become
because things we have done
are redone
and redone.

We hardly notice the rinsing
of a cup, the drinking of coffee.

I seek sanctuary from
the crimes time commits
by switching rooms,
waking into a different day,
upsetting the order of things,
throwing the known away.

A Mayfly's life is a party,
an orgy, a Festival of Flies–
I have lived tens of thousands
of Mayfly lives, few
a celebration of birth and death
as theirs.

Today, this day, you are coming by.
We will talk, laugh, argue,
make love, watch the branches

shift in the wind, the shadows
pattern the wall.

We will have our day–
not a day of Mayflies, but
we will have our day, and time
will be stayed
while I memorize the openings
and closings
of your eyes.

*Peter Martori enjoys the poetry community in the Four Corners area,
the open mics and workshops. Meeting a diverse group of talented poets has
rekindled his desire to write and share how he sees the world with others.*

Cell Phone

Grace Morledge

There's no warning when my mind scrolls back to the minute Raoul was taken. It's like they take him all over again, like God wants to make me crazy. Gramp confiscated my phone when I broke the screen last week, so I can't even text anybody now. But in my head, there's a video on repeat.

It happened like this. I was sitting in Science, hot wind blasting through the windows, watching Jaylin Lambertson in cutoffs and a crop top painting her fingernails purple. I was loving her long brown legs and the way her smooth chest rounded just below her tan line when an elbow jabbed me. "Brady, write the data down."

"Yeah, I got it."

"No, you didn't. I moved the receiver. This is a new distance."

Raoul's the best lab partner because he gets things done, always has, since kindergarten. I was recording our readings to see how strong a wireless signal stayed over distance, that is until Jaylin stood up and vamped towards the pencil sharpener, heels snapping glittery flip-flops. Raoul grabbed my arm and shook me. I looked into his face: the brown eyes, the weird downward point of his hair-line, the "Let's get this done" grin saying we'd raise some hell later on. Gramp says Raoul knows me like the back of his hand.

Something hit the classroom door hard. Mrs. Harrell jerked and pulled off her reading glasses. A second bang landed louder, thrumming the metal. "Are those shots or rocks?" I asked.

"Oh shit," Raoul whispered.

Time gained speed as two men crashed in, helmets and Kevlar vests, neck wraps over their noses, ICE stamped across their chests like on TV, slamming the door against the wall. Mrs. Harrell jumped up out of her chair. Jaylin screamed. The tall guy cradling a long gun stomped to Harrell's desk and mispronounced the names of people I knew – loud, like they'd wronged him personally.

"We're here for Raul Gitterez. Son of Concha and Hosay Git-terez."

"Raoul Guitterez?" Mrs. Harrell's voice soared like a girl's. She looked scared shitless, like I'd never seen her, her face paper-white and all her acne scars glowing like LEDs.

"That's the kid. Where is he?" The tall man shoved a paper in Harrell's face. She grabbed it and reached for her glasses.

"He's . . . not here today." That was brave, but they weren't buy-ing it.

"Bullshit," said the tall man. "The office said he's in this room."

I glimpsed Raoul, all our years of friendship slicing me as Harrell pointed at us, and because he wasn't after a red-haired kid with blue eyes, ICE Man grabbed my bro. His helper zip-tied Raoul's hands and they flung him out the door before he could scream, so his desperate wail only echoed down the hall. Jaylin sobbed, and the kids ran to the windows, and after that things went insane for a while.

You see, Raoul James Guitterez is an American citizen. He was born here, but they took him right off his lab stool in seventh grade Science at Mitchell Middle School, two days ahead of summer vacation.

And I have his backpack.

It's under my bed. I don't know how I got out of class with it, but the Science lab ended after what happened, happened. People were yelling and crying, and Harrell called Principal Barnes on her cell phone and he charged in just as the bell rang, when I grabbed Raoul's pack and mine and threw them both over my shoulder. I walked out the front door of the school, and then I started to run, and I ran all the way to my house where I paced the weedy yard for an hour, sweating, my heart hammering. Nobody noticed I'd left school. It was like a bomb had gone off in that place. Then God tapped the arrow on my head screen, and since then he hasn't hit pause.

When Gramp gets home from work, I know that he knows what's happened. It made the Denver news, because I checked, the reporter talking seriously outside my school. They must have flown her down.

Gramp slumps in his La-Z-Boy, pulls off his boots and his landscaper's hat, and rubs his hands through his orange-white hair to loosen the sweat. Then he looks at me.

"You know that kid?" The two of us don't waste words.

"He's my best friend."

Gramp's eyes get big, the only way I know he feels me. "That was Raoul?"

"They took him out of Science class." My throat stiffens with tears that want out, but I can't let them go. Not here, not now.

"Damn," Gramp says. "Damn it." That's all, and then after a minute he tells me, "You better get the lawn mowed tonight. It'll rain tomorrow."

God keeps replaying the video while I mow and while I choke

down the burger Gramp has grilled, and while I shower off the grass clippings. In the bathroom, water running hot and loud, I let myself cry a little. I feel better after that, for a while. In the living room, Gramp is watching the news. Raoul's school picture is up there now. "ICE Detains American Student."

"Do they know where he is?" I ask.

"No. They think maybe the Aurora Detention Center."

"Why? He's American. The news woman says so."

"That's what he told people," Gramp says. "Maybe he lied."

"Raoul?"

He doesn't answer. It hurts. Gramp has known Raoul as long as I have. A screen crawl keeps rerunning the station's tip line number. It hits me that everybody's clueless. Maybe not even ICE knows where he is.

After a minute I say, "I'm not going back to school."

"Your grades in?" Gramp asks.

"Yeah."

He shrugs. "Then it's all the same to me. But you can't start the weeding job until after Memorial Day."

"I know that."

"Behave yourself."

I guess I'm free, except for the video in my head.

God keeps messing with me because of Grandma, who used to take me to the Lutheran church. She died of breast cancer when I was eight-and-a-half. I've been trying to shake God's company since, but when shit goes down, he won't let me alone. While he's hanging out, I wish he'd give me some advice because Raoul's alive and I don't know where and that's worse than if he were dead somehow.

I last see the clock at 4:12 a.m., then I jump awake when Gramp revs up his work truck. Though my head's full of tired haze, I feel the backpack where it's hiding. I pour a bowl of cereal that tastes like cardboard and crash on the couch in my shorts for an hour or two, watching the rain start and stop and listening to thunder rumbling miles away. After the first couple news reports, I mute the TV. When the news people try to get info, the feds don't answer, so they tell another pointless story. I turn on the Xbox, but I can't focus, so I throw on my work shorts and old Nuggets t-shirt and make my bed because Gramp will check it. The backpack. I lie on my belly and reach among the dust wads and pull it into my room. It's red and dirty, marked with ink spots and ballpoint tattoo designs and a slit in the outside zipper pouch where I slashed it with my folding knife when I got mad at Raoul for telling Jaylin I think she's fine.

He got me back right away. He tied a piece of her hair into the zipper loop of my pack. How he got hold of it I don't know, but it was for sure her hair. Dark blonde with purple streaks. Gramp says Raoul could talk the hide off a snake, so I bet he got her to cut it off herself. He tied it with one of his crazy knots and closed the zipper on it enough times that I'd never get that hair loose again. Raoul said it was a Rapunzel lock, and I was stuck with it.

The memory cuts me, and my eyes burn, and suddenly I'm furious – at the feds, and at Gramp for disbelieving, and at Harrell for being gutless, and at Raoul for having illegal parents. I throw the backpack across the room where it smacks with a thud against a dresser drawer. Then I feel bad. "God, I'm not mad at Raoul," I say, which is partly true.

Out of the slit in the zipper pouch, Raoul's cell phone slides onto the floor.

His phone. I rub my lying eyes. He always kept it in his pocket, never in the pack where it could get lost or stolen. The first thing ICE Man probably did once they were down the hall was to frisk him and confiscate his electronics. But no. The phone is there, flat on the floor in its silver case. Did he put it in the pack when he knew they were coming? Did he and his parents sit around talking about what he'd do if ICE came after him? Had he always known they might? Had he just been waiting for it?

I spring across the room and grab the phone. The screen is dark, showing only Raoul's fingerprints. He would have turned it off when he'd hid it, but I know his passcode. It's his birthday. No, the phone is truly dead. It's an old iPhone and mine, when I had one, was a Samsung. I'll need an Apple charger. They might have them at Wal-Mart, but not for six bucks, which is all the mowing money I have left. I shake the phone like it's a dying animal that might come back to life. Then I think of Jaylin. She has an Apple smartphone, and I don't know her number, of course, but she lives down on Eighth, off Gulch Road. I'll take the bus. School's out soon. It's a workday for teachers. My thoughts spin and the kidnapping video cues up. That's what it was, a kidnapping. God, I think, don't make me watch it now. And he doesn't.

I throw the red backpack under my bed and slide Raoul's phone into the inner pocket of my pack. I scrounge some coins from the change pot in the kitchen. It's 11:05. I don't know what to tell Jaylin, but she saw what I saw, so maybe she gets it. I run four blocks to the stop where the bus is idling and the door flies open and I jump up the stairs, drop my coins in the slot, slide into a window seat. Two old ladies across the aisle are talking about a road work detour. "It's just ridiculous," one of them says. "How many times are they going to tear up this road?"

The video rolls, and hard as I try, I can't pause it. Last Science lab of the year – a fun one and expensive, Mrs. Harrell said. And me watching Jaylin so that Raoul had to pull me on task. Then the bangs, and my voice saying, "A shot or a rock?" and Raoul's "Oh shit," and Harrell's cowardliness and Jaylin's scream. "How many times are they going to tear up this road?"

She died without saying a word, thin as nothing in the living room hospital bed with just me there, clutching the bed rail. Gramp had gone out to grab a smoke before the hospice lady came, which takes forever when you're eight. Grandma looked asleep, but once Gramp was gone, her eyes opened part way, and they were murky blue with a dead-fish fog. Her mouth went sideways, caked with white spit. I started to bawl as she did her dying, keeping those fish eyes on me, and I wasn't allowed to look away, so I watched until the hospice lady knocked and then rattled the door and walked on in. She marked me with a look, annoyed and sorry, then slid the stethoscope from her neck and laid it on Grandma's chest. "Where's your grandpa?"

"I don't know."

"Men step out." She put on a sad smile and said she was sorry, but that my grandmother was dead.

I didn't need her to tell me that.

When I get off the bus at the 8th Avenue stop, traffic is pretty heavy, and the spring wind is blowing up more rain clouds. I walk alongside the old wire fence beside the squat brown house where I know Jaylin lives. Only in my dreams has she ever been out in her yard, but today she is there, sitting on her knees yanking weeds out of a flower bed like a crazy person.

"Jaylin?"

"What?" She sounds mad until she sees who it is. She stands up, pushing the blonde and purple hair off her forehead. Her face is red and swollen.

I swallow. "Have you got an iPhone charger?" I hold up Raoul's phone.

"That's his. I recognize the silver case." Her red eyes fill and her nose is dripping. She wipes it with her arm, and I know that Jaylin will never love *me*. How stupid am I? "Come inside," she says.

Jaylin's living room is dark, with the curtains closed against the heat. She flops down on the end of a sagging sectional and plugs Raoul's phone into the white cord that lies on the arm rest. We watch the empty battery icon appear. That phone is good and dead.

"Where'd you get this?"

"I took his backpack."

"Hah! Barnes and Harrell trashed the Science room looking for it."

"His was next to mine, so I grabbed it. I left when the bell rang."

She doesn't offer, but I sit beside her and drop my backpack on the floor between us – a mistake. When Jaylin spots her hair tangled up in the zipper, there's a look on her face like she's been kicked in the gut. Her mouth twists, tears pour down, and she starts to cry big, ragged sobs like nobody does unless they mean it. I get that she gave Raoul that hair on her own. What do you do when a girl starts crying like that and it's not about you?

I pat her arm.

Then the phone begins to ping, and ping, and ping. Jaylin grabs it and scrolls through the texts my friend has been sending for hours. They come thick and fast, and I feel joyful that Raoul is out there texting, and jealous that Jaylin is reading his thoughts.

"What's he say? Tell me."

"He's in detention."

"In Aurora?"

"Yeah."

"Is he coming back?"

Smeared with snot and with her hair all sweaty, she looks straight at me for the first time. "What do *you* think?" I've never heard Jaylin sound so sarcastic about anything actually important.

"But he's an American," I say.

"But they've got his parents. Who'd take care of him? Where'd he stay? It's so fucked up." Jaylin slides off the couch onto the floor with her knees bent and her head on her folded arms, like a turtle.

"Can I see the phone?" When she doesn't answer, I wait a minute, then reach out and slide it from her fingers.

I type in Raoul's birthday and scroll through the texts he's sent himself from a number I don't know. They are full of his voice. He's in a cell with a bunch of men, but not his parents. Somehow, someone has a burner phone.

"Raoul," I text. "It's Brady"

"*Laughing/crying emoji face*. No shit you got my phone!"

"I took your backpack"

"Bro you rock! Passport inside pocket"

"Yours?"

"Duh!"

"I've got his passport," I tell Jaylin. She stares at me, confused. "In his backpack."

"Wow," she mouths at me.

"Who gets it?" I text Raoul.

"Not Barnes."

The news tip-line banner scrolls into my head. "I've got a news reporter number."

"Great," he texts. "Got to go." And Raoul is gone.

I don't talk on phones, but this is an emergency. I tap in the number, and it rings once. Then a woman's voice answers with her name—Dawn something—and the station's call letters. I take a dry swallow to get my voice moving.

"Hello, miss. I've got Raoul Guitterez's passport."

There's a moment. "Could you tell me your name, please?"

There's Gramp, and then there's God. I almost hang up.

"Brady Cavanaugh," I say. "I'm his friend. He left it with me to keep safe."

"How old are you?"

"Thirteen." Well, in August.

"Do you have a parent I can talk to?"

My head reel shows me Gramp in his recliner, sweaty and tired. "Behave yourself," he says.

"No," I say to Dawn.

"What's happening?" Jaylin asks. I wave her voice away.

"I talked to him," I say into Raoul's cell phone. "He's in a cell in Aurora alone with a bunch of men."

There's a gasp. "Look, Brady. I'll need to see that passport and talk to you, to get more information. Where can I meet you?"

I see the backpack in my room, by the dresser, the passport inside. Gramp is gone, but he'll know. He'll know.

"Here's my home address," I say to this stranger that I've called on Raoul's cell phone.

God, help me now, I think. Or I pray. I'm going with you.

Grace Morledge has worked with words all her life as a library and archival assistant, journalist, and teacher of English and creative writing. She has lived in Durango since 2020. She is presently working on a novel set in a near-future Southwest that is proving to be dishearteningly prophetic.

Deesdoi: a summer album

Danielle Shandiin Emerson

Tan, cheap fabric against my cheek, lying parallel to the
hot dashboard in the back seat, radio silent, dying—kinda.

     I pull my feet up to my chest, practicing the once fun ol'
     swimming cannonball my taller cuzzins reminisce about.

The AC is busted—*it never worked & never will*, he says.
Shizhe'é drives the highways with windows rolled down.

     Lukewarm sheets of air move like hands, supple through
     tangled hair 'til I can't see anything—ádin—beyond shí

choppy bangs, kissing that unexpected 45-degree angle cut
with sticky palms; a pair of shimasaní's sewing box scissors.

     Snip. Chop. Snip. Snip. Chop. Snip. *Shhh. Shhh. Shhhhhhh.*
     Shizhe'é sits with one arm on the sill, unfazed exhaust-tion.

Sweat collects in sand pools on shí nose & upper lip, within
reach of my tongue, lassoing 'round shí molars, pink & red.

I swipe at it. Twice. *Bitter áshįįh*, I sing. Cheii taught me that word.
Swelt silence becomes a kind of summer music. Clenched & wrung

tight like new guitar strings, then strummed care-lessly until
snapping; thin juniper branches broken in half by tight knees.

Shí dóó shizhe'é will cascade yellow & black, extracted then
distributed against our will, dying—kinda, in a wise, old heat

that just keeps getting wiser & older until—at last—
it outlives us all.

*Danielle Shandiin Emerson is a Diné writer from Shiprock on the Na-
vajo Nation. Her clans are Tłaashchi'i* (Red Cheek People Clan), born
for *Ta'neezaahnii* (Tangled People Clan). Her maternal grandfather is
*Ashįįhí (Salt People Clan) and her paternal grandfather is Táchii'nii (Red
Running into the Water People Clan). She has a B.A. in Education Studies
and a B.A. in Literary Arts from Brown University.*

Rainbearers

Michael Engelhard

A drum steady as a metronome announces the procession. The still February air buzzes with anticipation, and my goose bumps are not from the cold. I am packed shoulder to shoulder with raven-haired people on a flat roof in Muh-oon-qah-pi, the "Place of Running Water," waiting to fall out of time.

Owl hoots join the drum, and then hail on flagstones—rattling from deer hooves, seeds, turtle shells. Here they come! A crush of masked bodies clad in the land's minerals, bright as hummingbirds, feathers and furs swaying, pounding bare ground with bare feet, inflating cloud bellows and bringing up seedlings with each stomp. This is Powamyua, the start of the Hopi ceremonial year and first appearance of the katsina spirits since their winter retreat to the San Francisco Peaks outside of Flagstaff.

I am in Moenkopi with a few river guides and Grand Canyon National Park staff as part of a collaborative arrangement between the park, river outfitters, and tribal groups. Through cultural immersion, this program seeks to increase our understanding of tribes affiliated with the canyon. Its practical goal is to enrich the interpretation of a cultural landscape by including First Peoples' perspectives.

Fortunately, we are not on our own. William Talashoma, a river guide and interpreter from Moenkopi, shepherds us through the maze of Hopi etiquette and beliefs. For a change, we guides are the guided ones, feeling like babes in the desert. On our way to the village, we briefly stopped at Cameron, near the lip of the Little Colorado River's gorge. There, William recounted his people's emergence from previous worlds, destroyed by ice, fire, and flood, into this present and final one. The place of emergence lies down canyon, near the confluence with the Colorado, where a travertine dome housing a spring swells from the riverbank like an earthen breast. Its Hopi name, Sipapuni, translates as "navel" or "umbilical cord." William thinks of it as a symbol of rebirth highlighting the fact that, like all of our food, we come from the earth. The Sipapuni evokes our ascent from primordial muck to consciousness. Fittingly, the souls of the dead return to this gateway for their journey home. As a navigational landmark, it pegs the tribe's surfacing from the canyon's depths onto the mesa tops after epic migrations across the Southwest that followed its last emergence.

At Moenkopi, we parked our van bumper to bumper with cars by the side of a congested dirt road. Down that road, single-story houses hunkered between tan bluffs and the wash's dormant cornfields. We followed a trickle of visitors toward the lower village, to the cottonwood-shaded spring that gave the village its name and still gives it life. Offerings had been left in a shrine-like niche: turkey feathers tied with white cotton string. A broken rattle. Yellow cornmeal. Carved prayer sticks, both male and female kinds, painted turquoise. I stooped to pick up a gray, corrugated potsherd that could have been a thousand years old. Though Moenkopi only dates back to 1870, the Hopis' Motsinom ancestors probably worshipped there.

As portals to the spirit world, springs did and still do hold meaning for people of the corn. We shared lunch with William's family, eating in shifts, as the house was bursting with guests. On the porch, a boy played with a painted bow, a gift from the elemental beings, the katsinas. We sat at a lunch counter where we were served *piki*— phyllo-thin blue corn bread baked on a heated stone slab. A girl with almond eyes and a shy smile warned me of the batch spiced with chilies. There was fry bread and beef soup with bean sprouts grown from heirloom varieties for the occasion in the underground secrecy of kivas, the clans' ceremonial chambers. Laughter erupted from the table around which elders and close family sat. In a dimly lit corner, an old-timer with mahogany skin reclined in a hospital bed, part of the proceedings.

Corn, like the Sipapuni, situates the Hopi in the cosmos. Cornmeal paths radiate outward from the origin place, with ears of various colors associated with the directions: yellow corn for the Northwest, blue corn with the Southwest, red corn with the Southeast, white corn with the Northeast, black corn with the Above, and multi-colored corn with the Below. How poor by comparison is our placeless Monsanto-designed variety.

Food should nourish the soul as well as the body, but too often nowadays, we ignore the spiritually sustaining for the merely nutritious, the profitable, or the faddish. The feast in this pueblo also was a reminder that food is about community, hospitality, obligations. Food simply cannot be separated from its social context.

The Powamyua, or "Bean Dance," concludes a 16-day ceremony of creation. The katsinas have arrived in force, helping the Hopis prepare for the growing season, and if the rituals are performed humbly and correctly, they will bring rain from the sacred peaks to the south. At the same time, it marks the initiation of young children into the entry-level Katsina Society, preparing yet another generation for growth and maturity. The Hopis, for whom the world teems with sentient beings, would not be surprised to hear of scientists' recent findings that tomatoes and tobacco plants shaken by drought or suddenly wounded emit staccato ultrasounds resembling bubble-wrap popping. The audible response, likely physiological, may stem from cavitation in the plants' tissues. But is a person's gasp of fear any less physical? These plant "distress cries" differ depending on the cause and may even affect nearby insects and other animals.

Like the planet's progress solemnized in this hilltop community, my journeying has come full circle. New to the country in 1983, I was hitchhiking across the Southwest when a Hopi who offered a ride invited me to visit with his family on Third Mesa. I stayed at his grandmother's house for a few days. A potter from the renowned Nampeyo lineage, she red pots the traditional way, burying redware smooth as calabashes and webbed with black geometric designs to smolder on cedar logs inside a mound of dry sheep manure. Her grandson painted watercolors of katsinas in lifelike poses, and I bought a set, which now hangs in my study. That Hopi family's kindness helped kindle a decades-long love affair with the Colorado Plateau and fed an interest in the continent's first people that eventually led me to anthropology and north, to Alaska.

From the rooftop, I see initiates wearing nothing but blankets, who stand with their godparent sponsors, sleep-deprived and hungry from their ordeal. Their near-nakedness signals humility, their bare feet a debt owed to the earth. They spent last night curled fetus-like in the kiva's womb, below a cornmeal line painted on the wall—the path that Maasawu, the Creator, expects them to follow. On the previous day, the katsinas had whipped them. When tears flushed their eyes, their godfathers had traded places with them, receiving the blows in their stead. This, too, a promise: if you walk the straight path, Maasawu will take on part of your suffering. Blood shed in this covenant is thicker than water.

The Mudhead chorus now marches past with its dried-clay masks, heads smooth as urns, eyes and mouths O-shaped, as if in constant surprise. Their big-bellied drum hums in the pit of my stomach. In tune with the fertility theme, clown katsinas pretend to hump old women in the crowd. Black ogres chase Hopi tough guys, trying to blacken their faces with soot. Other monsters go from door to door, threatening to eat children who have misbehaved, and demanding fresh meat. Spectators who line the streets pluck feathers from the procession's wake, blessings the katsinas left in the dirt. Humor and horseplay, mixed with awe and reverence, take me by surprise. What I witness shows me that the sacred and the profane are as much part of a continuum in an eddying universe as the seasons and generations.

Katsinas circle the village four times, always, *always* following the sun's daily and annual course. (We'd call it "clockwise," but abstract time, time detached from the body, has no function in rites linked to the earth.) The dancers stop on every kiva roof, where the clan priests consecrate them with cornmeal, "feeding" the spirits that have traveled so far. With each round, I recognize more characters in the melee of colors and forms.

A Kokopelli Katsina—"a nympho," according to William—sports a woman's kilt and the Hopi woman's twin-whorl sculpted "butterfly" hairdo.

A Mocking Katsina latches onto bystanders and the ranks of fellow katsinas, mimicking his target's every move. Dressed in cutoff jeans, modern footwear, hippie pendants, and a beaded vest, he resembles certain White Men.

A Guard Katsina in a checkered kilt points its yucca wand at me. Guards punish any transgression on the katsinas' path, and it takes me a few seconds and the example of others on the roof to understand the request to remove my cap.

A Heheya Katsina with a lasso tempts children by holding out woven baskets, katsina dolls, bundles of *piki*, or cookies on a string, snaring them when they reach for his gifts. This tempting with riches, and the white-plumed, spruce-ruffed Snow Katsina, bring to mind a controversy that embroils my one-time hometown, Flagstaff, an hour from here as the vulture soars. A ski resort operator plans to use wastewater to supply the barren slopes of the San Francisco Peaks with snow there. Concerned residents, environmental organizations, and Hopi representatives have protested such waste and desecration; but it looks as if the city will go ahead anyhow.

The range on the south rim of the Colorado Plateau, comprised in the Kachina Peaks Wilderness, is Nuvatukya'ovi, the "Place of the High Snows." Sadly, that name no longer seems appropriate. One of the deities to whom it is home is Nuvak'chin Mana, in charge of cold weather and the white gift that saturates earth for the next year's crops.

Could the multi-year drought that squeezes the West signal our straying from ground truths, from the straight path? Have we lost sight of priorities in a desert? Dancing for harmony in the world, the pueblos are dancing for all of us.

These days, wastewater snow for a Flagstaff ski resort defiles the peaks' hallowed flanks. Many Hopis condemn snowmaking itself as sacrilegious, since it interferes with the natural water cycle. The effluent of the affluent includes runoff from mortuaries and hospitals, associated with death, disease, and spiritual contamination. One member of the tribe compared the practice to "urinating on the altar at the Vatican," and anthropologists to baptizing babies with dishwater. The Grand Canyon's Hualapai fear that vile meltwater will seep into the ground and from there percolate into a sacred spring below the Snowbowl. Indigenous Mountain Protectors from an inter-tribal alliance, praying and protesting at the resort, have been insulted, attacked by snowboarders, and arrested. For these tableland dwellers, springs and their source are linked to the health of the world and all things living in it. Like certain shrines, ruins, trail cairns, and petroglyphs, ceremonial springs are "footprints" that Hopi ancestors left behind on their wanderings to the center place. Spring water is "wild water," in which benevolent water serpents dwell.

A katsina song that Emory Sekaquaptewa, the "Noah Webster of the Hopi nation," recalled offers a mesa perspective:

They are preparing themselves,
Over there at the snow-capped mountains.
The clouds,
From there, they are putting on their endowments,
To come here.

Hopi women, children, and men, after death, become clouds.

Skiers as well, and backpackers and river runners, should understand the katsinas' cargo, those blessings from the departed, as a divine endowment.

Toward evening, we drive on to Shongopavi, perched on a spur of Second Mesa. Residents of Old Shongopavi relocated here after the Pueblo uprising of 1680, fearing Apache marauders and reprisals from the Spanish. Outside ideas, diseases, and trappings have taken their toll, but this village remains a stronghold of Hopi tradition. We shiver in sweaters and pile jackets, while the supplicants brave the late winter chill bare-chested. There is less levity here, less chasing and teasing. Despite our lighter skin and self-conscious poses, nobody pays us any attention. A different cast of katsinas shuffles through Shongopavi's still-frozen mud, dwarfed by the wing-helmeted, somber Crow Mother. Yowe, the katsina that beheaded the Franciscan priest more than 300 years ago, wields an old saber. Memory runs deep on the mesas, as does the desire for restoration. A few people in the audience ask for canings, to be cleansed and healed. It feels like a foreign place at the heart of America. But no. This *is* the ancient heart of America—wounded but resilient, vibrant, enduring, powered by and powering immemorial cycles.

In a handout for the trip's participants, William had summarized the Hopi worldview. "We must have constant prayer in our hearts, from the minute we are awake till the time we are asleep. We must respect both the spirit and the creation."

"Hopi," William said at one point, "is not a tribe, but a state of being."

At last light, the main kiva swallows the host of katsinas. One by one, their feathered silhouettes shrink into the roof hatch. Eventually, only the tip of the ladder that they descended protrudes aboveground, angled at the first stars. The rooftops and streets quickly empty. As we walk back to the dirt parking lot, a TV like a blue eye flickers from a dark house with a satellite dish.

Trained as a cultural anthropologist, Michael Engelhard worked 25 years as a wilderness guide and outdoor educator in the canyon country and arctic Alaska. His latest books include the memoir Arctic Traverse *and the collection of canyon essays* No Walk in the Park. *He currently lives in Moab, Utah, again.*

MANIFEST

Benjamin Green

Next day, nothing seemed in place,
nothing resolved,
the soil in his garden only
felt like dirt touching fingertips.

The desert formed a metaphor
for *the void*, but remained
the one place *God,*
whatever the spirit's name,
could walk in peace,

where what connects, what makes a through-line,
becomes, *and* unbecomes.

He became, gradually,
the old man who knew

the weight of sky
and the thirst of soil;
the old man who tried
to account for his solitude:

thinking how the gap between
lightning and thunder
resembles the eternity
between intention and action,
how insight and understanding
fade like smoke in wind
or water flowing through fingers

(and yet he *knows*
how water manifests into
the beauty
of a cutthroat trout).

Benjamin Green is the author of eleven books, including The Sound of Fish Dreaming *(Bellowing Ark Press, 1996) and the upcoming* Old Man Looking through a Window at Night *(Main Street Rag) and* His Only Merit *(Finishing Line Press). At the age of sixty-nine, he hopes his new work articulates a mature vision of the world and does so with some integrity. He resides in Jemez Springs.*

Trina

TJ Patton

Something sharp poked into the bottom of her foot, and Trina swore softly, not wanting to offend the old lady in the kitchen. She kicked at the culprit, a chunk of dried mud.

The mud room certainly lived up to its name. There were more than a dozen pairs of boots and shoes in various sizes, all muddy to one degree or another. The hooks on the wall held enough flannels, zippered hoodies, and canvas farm coats to stock a small thrift store.

Trina chose a purple sweatshirt because it wasn't black or navy or tan like everything else in here. She pulled a black canvas coat over the sweatshirt, stepped her size eight feet into size ten rubber boots, and opened the back door only to be greeted by fifteen degrees of hell-hath-frozen-over.

Morning light sparkled off the icicles dangling from the gutters. Snow covered the hills in every direction. Abel Acres was six hours south of Denver by car. It was cold in the city too, but days like this were meant for staying indoors. Or, if she had to go out, being in the car with the heat on full blast, wearing her calf-length lavender down coat. She loved that coat. She missed that coat.

It was a gift from Don. He enjoyed giving her pretty clothes and expensive jewelry, and he had good taste. It was one of his better qualities.

What would he think if he could see her now? Bundled up in bulky, ugly clothes that had been worn by God only knew how many other unlucky women, hiding in this dilapidated old farm-house, trudging through four inches of fresh snow on her way to a goat pen.

A *goat* pen.

She, a city girl through and through. Trina dreamt of penthouses, not henhouses, and certainly not goat pens.

If she'd known that one desperate phone call would land her here, would she still have made it? At this moment, before coffee and breakfast, with the wind already numbing her face, she could not honestly say yes.

Not that anyone was asking.

Her own friends had gone to the wayside one by one since she'd moved in with Don, and her disapproving family had left it up to her to call them these days. The friends she shared with Don would believe whatever he told them. He could be very persuasive.

Never in her life had she felt so alone.

The people here said they could help her, and she did appreciate that, but it's not like they weren't asking anything in return. Chores are required, they said. Trina had expected a bit of light housework, but nothing like this.

She pulled open the gate and entered the pen, hungry goats bleating at her and swarming her legs. So many goats. Black ones, brown ones, white ones, with horns and without. Some big and some small, but no babies. Kids, as she now knew they were called, were in the next pen with the mamas.

The ones surrounding her were all begging for food.

"Yeah, I get it, you're hungry. So am I."

Michelle had shown Trina where the food was the day before. A big woman with brown skin, somewhere in her middle forties, Michelle was the one who had picked Trina up at the mini mart at three a.m. and brought her out here. Trina's car, a gift from Don, had his name on the title, not hers. He wouldn't have reported it stolen because cops were the last people he'd want to deal with, but even if she'd been in any condition to drive herself, Trina wouldn't have dared take the Mustang. It would have given him one more reason to track her down.

She scooped oats out of the bin, hearing Michelle's instructions.

They get hay and extra oats to fatten them up.

Why fatten them? Trina asked.

They're meat goats.

Trina shuddered, and Michelle laughed.

I didn't know people ate goats.

People will eat anything if they're hungry enough. Goat's not bad, but it is a bit gamey, kinda like venison.

Gross. No venison or goat for me, thank you.

I hate to tell you this, Michelle smiled in a way that indicated the opposite, but Bette's breakfast sausage is made of goat meat.

No wonder she'd felt queasy after breakfast yesterday. Feeling tricked, Trina had made a mental vow to avoid meat while she was here.

As she filled the troughs with hay and added the oats, Trina thought again about the lavender coat hanging in her closet. How long until Don got rid of her clothes? Would he let Brit go through her stuff and take what she wanted? A friend of Don's sister, Brit spent a lot of time at the house and made no secret of coveting everything that belonged to Trina, including Don.

Trina still had a house key in her purse. She'd go in while Don was at work. She'd clean the place, as it would certainly be a mess, and then she'd order take-out Chinese food, which was his favorite. Dinner would be waiting when he got home. She'd slip right back into her old life as if she'd never left.

Sober, Don would be happy to see her. He'd apologize for losing his temper, and he'd promise that things would be different this time. These were all things he'd said before, but one thing was already different this time–she'd never left before. Now that he knew she had the guts to leave him, he'd realize that it was him who had to change. He'd have to treat her better if he wanted her to stay.

Trina made her way into the birthing pen.

The mama goat and her new kid looked cozy enough, settled in a bed of straw. Wilma F. is what Michelle said her name was. The old lady named her goat after Wilma Flintstone due to the tuft of red hair that stuck up on her head.

Trina knelt next to the goat and stroked the tuft, smoothing it down. A memory came back to her, a conversation between her mother and grandmother about the Flintstones, a prehistoric cartoon family. Her grandma defended the show, saying that Fred was flawed but basically a good person, while Trina's mother insisted that Fred was a typical bad-tempered man-boy and that Wilma could do better.

Trina gave the baby a gentle pet and spoke soothingly to Wilma F. "It must be nice, not having to deal with the billy goat who knocked you up. You get to rest in peace with your baby."

Rest in peace.

Maybe not the best choice of words.

Trina pushed her tongue into the space where one of her front teeth used to be. Don owed it to her to fix this. She'd make it a condition of her coming home.

Thoughts far away, Trina headed for the chicken coop.

The smell of sausage hit her the moment she stepped into the kitchen. She brought her hand to her mouth and looked around for a place to vomit. Fortunately it was a false alarm and only a dry heave.

The kitchen had deep double sinks, and no dishwasher. Cast-iron pots hung on nails on the wall, down low so Bette could reach them. A tiny, white-haired woman in her seventies, Bette, wearing baggy jeans and an old wool sweater with a hole in it, stood at the stove stirring oats.

"How's Wilma this morning?"

"She seemed fine to me." *But what do I know about goats? Or being a new mom?*

"This will be her last kid. She's getting old."

"What's considered old in goat years?"

"She's ten now, and she'll probably live another five to eight years."

"How many babies—kids—has she had?"

"This is number ten."

"One a year. Sounds like hell to me."

"She had twins twice."

"Even worse." Trina's hand went to her belly.

Bette noticed. "Feeling okay?"

"Yeah, I'm all right. It's just that the smell of the sausage is getting to me."

Bette nodded. "The oatmeal might sit better. It's ready if you want to serve yourself."

Trina remembered what Michelle had said about using oats to fatten up the goats. Don always noticed when she gained weight, even a couple pounds. There was no way to stop it now, so she might as well enjoy the oatmeal. She filled her bowl, added raisins, almonds, cinnamon, and honey, and sat down at the battered wooden table.

It looked more like an outdoor table than an indoor one, and it was long enough to seat six with a bench against the wall. There were messages carved into the table. Right next to her bowl were the words: Thanks Bette, you're an angel, A.G.

Bette sat across from her. She looked child-sized, but her face was far from youthful. Deep lines stretched from her eyes to her jaw. Her coloring was a permanent brown, the kind you get from living your life too close to the sun. Her eyes were a bright and sparkly blue, her short hair as white as paper.

"I got you an appointment with a dentist to have a bridge put in."

"A bridge, not implants?"

"I haven't found a surgeon willing to do implants for free. They're too expensive."

Trina flushed, embarrassed to have sounded ungrateful. She was a charity case, after all. But a bridge meant having two good teeth whittled down to stubs to support the fake tooth. Implants were more like real teeth. Don could afford implants. If she asked in exactly the right way, and if she took on some of the blame—admitted she shouldn't have said what she said, especially not when he'd been drinking—would he offer to pay?

If she came back, he'd want her to be pretty again.

"I have a lead on a receptionist job in Cortez. Doesn't pay much, but it's a start."

Trina thought again of her full closet. "I'll have to go back and get my clothes."

Bette frowned, causing the lines that flared out from the sides of her eyes to deepen. "Do you think that's a good idea?"

"If I go when he's at work it'll be fine."

"You said before that he comes home at random times during the day."

"I can't just leave everything behind."

"I'd suggest you have a police officer go with you, but you've said that isn't an option."

"It's not." If the cops showed up at his door, if they searched the place, Don would make good on his threat to accuse *her* of theft. The coats and jewelry were only the tip of the iceberg. Now that she knew the truth of where the gifts and all his extra income came from, she wouldn't be able to lie convincingly.

Who would believe you? Brit will back my story, not yours. You know that, right?

She did know it. She knew too much now, and that was the problem. Or one of the problems. If only she'd handled it better when she'd found out and not threatened to report him. If, instead of yelling and making Don feel bad—men had such fragile egos—she'd assured him that she was content with what he earned working construction. She didn't need fancy stuff. He was enough. Together, they had everything they needed to live a good life and start a family together. If she'd stayed calm, he might have listened to her and she wouldn't have had to leave.

"I know a place that gives out vouchers for a couple of outfits. Not new, but gently used, good for job interviews and work."

Trina nodded, barely aware that she'd stopped eating and was absently tracing the letters carved into the wood with her index finger.

"She's dead," Bette said.

"Who?"

"Alana Gavin. A.G."

Trina pulled her hand away from the letters as if dying was a virus she might catch.

"How?"

"Single bullet to the forehead."

Trina shuddered. "Her man found her?"

"He didn't have to look for her. She went back on her own."

"Why?"

"She wanted to give him one more chance for the sake of the kids. They had two boys, seven and nine. They missed their father."

"I see."

"So did they. He made them watch."

"Jesus. Why are you telling me this?"

But she knew, of course she did. The answer was in Bette's blue eyes, eyes so intense that it hurt to look at them. Trina lowered her gaze, staring into her oatmeal.

After a moment, Trina brought a spoonful to her mouth. It had gone cold and was getting gluey. An almond got stuck in the raw spot where her tooth had been. She pushed it out with her tongue, flinching at the pain. The wound needed a bit more time to heal.

The nausea came roaring back. This time it wasn't a false alarm. She looked around, frantic.

A trash can appeared in front of her.

When Trina was finished, Bette pulled the string on the white trash sack, lifted it out of the container, and carried it outside.

Trina pushed the bowl of oatmeal to one side.

Bette came back inside. She opened the cupboard under the sink, retrieved a fresh trash sack, and inserted it in the container. She washed her hands.

"You mentioned a clinic," Trina said, one hand on her abdomen.

Bette sat back down at the table. "We can make you an appointment if that's what you want."

It wasn't, not really. None of this is what she wanted.

Bette's wrinkled, brown-spotted hand came to rest on Trina's smooth, unblemished one. "Whatever you decide, know that you're not alone."

It wasn't true.

Trina knew that she was alone in the same way that everyone is alone, trapped within their one and only body, living their one and only life, for good or for bad.

And yet, at that moment, she felt less alone than she had in a long time, and that certainly meant something.

TJ Patton divides her time between Southwest Colorado and the Pacific Northwest. "Trina" is from her upcoming series House of Hurt and is available, along with her other fiction, at tjpatton.substack.com.

THE SANDHILL SUMMER

Geneva Toland

In the cattle fields two sandhill cranes
nested last summer. I'd find them in the shade
and spray of the walking sprinkler, their wings redder
each day from the painting of mud and clay. By July
a babe walked with them, a small mirror of the others,
dipping neck to grass, picking cricket or worm, lifting
wing and leg to dance and croak. The town loved them wholly.
Facebook messenger chats announced every sighting—
each day a celebration. When they left in September,
we felt full—full of a summer spent in line at the grocery store
asking *did you see them?* and *how about the baby?*
The cattle stayed in the mountains a bit longer
so the fields lay empty for a while, except for the sprinklers
kept on in a desert valley where snow
is the only source for water, crop, life. It's complicated.
We believe in different worlds, different gods.

Pray to different futures and fear different yet similar deaths.
For a few months though, we were one town, one people
living in a mountain valley, searching the fields
for three long-necked miracles, wings spread red bright clay
to the sky.

Geneva Toland is currently working towards her MFA in Poetry at the Institute of American Indian Arts. She feels humbled to live in the home-lands of the Ute, Diné, and Puebloan peoples, where she teaches writing workshops, leads song circles, and plays with kids in the woods. See her other offerings at www.genevatoland.com.

The Wind

Lydia DeHaven

I am the wind. Look around us. All of this dirt was blown in by me. It's piled little orange-red pieces of sand eroded from ancient seas no human has seen and carried here from the west to shuffle into the formation of what we call soil and to create the foundation that holds my feet, holds my house, holds you swimming in my womb.

Every day with you, I walk on the soil of the little canyon beyond my backyard gate. The wind brings in the soil and erodes it away. I am the wind, I am nature, I am two heartbeats. My wind sends gusts of nutrients and spirit to you through a sinewy cord. It's pulsating. My wind erodes away my ego. Who was I before? What was I? Before this and before you?

I once thought children were the ultimate display of ego. Now I know they are the ultimate dissemination of self.

The people have said birth is the ocean, and the rhythm of the waves will bring emergence. I don't see the salty water. Where is it? How will you come?

I see the sun glistening off of sandstone resplendent in yellow hues and plumes of green lichen. I look southwest to see the bumps of the head, chest, and toes of the Sleeping Ute Mountain, the powerful warrior resting over our city. His nature changes slowly, my nature is fast-paced. You rest with him, rocked to sleep with each stride I take as my bump grows quickly.

The seasons are changing with us. The short days set in just as you start taking full occupancy of my body, expanding into the cracks and corners, making skin stretch and ripple. Eroding down my muscles with kicks, hiccups, and burps. A line starts to appear down the center of my stomach. It's the exit path from my heart to your homecoming.

We rest. It's dark early. We need the rest. During the long nights, you become a spirit. I become the wind. I wake up at 3 a.m. every day when the veil is thinnest at the portal of life and death. I can feel my ancestors. They are sending me messages. I listen in gratitude, one hand on my belly, one on my heart. The message ends, and I respond, "Thank you, baby, Thank you, body, Thank you, ancestors." Sleep resumes. Sometimes, when the ancestors are busy, you send me visions. We hold hands and walk into a spiral as you turn and whisper your name. You tell me it is time to focus, focus on us, focus on retrieving you from the portal. You will come when there is snow on the ground. I have asked you not to come at night. I am afraid of the dark. Will you help me? I need your help.

We are back on the soil in our little canyon beyond the back-yard gate. My feet are grounded. I look east, the tips of the La Plata Mountains grow white as you finish your formation, only needing to fatten up before emergence. The gray hairs on top of my head shine in the never-ending sun that winter cannot hide from our desert. There is no room for collagen in my once-dark brown locks. I have blown that energy down to you. My mind remembers a Ute Mountain Ute elder told me that after a baby is born, they take the placenta to the mountains so the baby always knows where their home is. You will always be home with me in our little canyon with the wind-blown soil under our feet.

I keep walking. I need to find more sticks to reinforce our nest to protect us from any negativity. The people keep asking me things and giving me emotions. Doesn't everyone see we are busy? Leave us alone. We are cocooned, I will not let the world distract us. You told me not to. I blow down the little backyard canyon, hoping to knock down more sticks to hide our vulnerability. There are not many sticks in our little canyon. I wonder how I can protect you with sage and sand, without water. It's a dry winter, my nose bleeds.

Focus, focus. We walk together. You are upside down, bouncing between bones. My feet grounded on the soil, when will the snow come? How many more times will we walk this little canyon as one?

The pain of life is in resistance. I hated the wind until I surrendered to it. Then, I became it. We walk down the little canyon to the mesa across from our neighborhood. I spread my arms, tears run down my face. I SURRENDER.

I am the wind. We are exposed, but the nest I have built around us is strong enough. I believe in it. I believe in you. I trust you will help me during your homecoming. Two ravens are above us, circling in and out. The wind carries the path their wings sail on. The turquoise sky provides them with perfect lighting for a daytime dance. Dance, ravens, dance. Then, in silence, they split and go separate ways, diving down to opposite sides of the little canyon. It's you and me, I cry. We are dancing in my wind. When the wind stops, we will be two.

Lydia DeHaven is redefining herself after the transformative birth of her second child. She proudly lives in Cortez, a place that called to her to make a home 13 years ago. She is an archaeologist and active community member who values the rich connections and history of the area.

Autorretrato

Jessica Pace

He is probably going out tonight.

Out into the dusk and the anonymity
and the circle and the rush

from the look on his face
lit with an ember still suggestible enough
to be stoked or extinguished
by the company one keeps.

Fortunately in 1923
like in any other time
passion bleeds warmly and blooms like a lit fuse,
a flower opening up in a dark room
when the rest of the world sleeps.

He is one of the ones who look for it everywhere,
insist on it,
even where it can't exist.
He should be proud of that –
for holding allegiance
to something other than daily life.

It lives in the space
between night sky and sinking sun.
It lives in plain sight, but on a ledge
and in the lungs, obviously,
where all reciprocity originates.
It lives in increments
and performs in short bursts
to make you think it was all a trick.

Of course, there is fear, too
and shame, maybe
and guilt, very likely.

But that's all part of the point.

Because *god* – I think –
at least he's got a real secret –
something so many of us
live our entire lives without.

Jessica Pace lives in the Four Corners. Her writing has been published in a smattering of literary journals.

Baahozhonii dóó gáh /
Baahozhonii & the Rabbit

Danielle Shandiin Emerson

aahozhonii's mother owned an art gallery. Not a fancy one. An art gallery that smelled like burnt toast and fried eggs on a hot summer morning. It filled noses, turning the air stale, even static, robbing travelers of their first breath. Every morning, the gallery stretched threaded string between skeleton fingers, taut with her mother's expectations. Cockroaches sought refuge in nooks, and stray cats snuck into shingled crevices on the roof. Baahozhonii heard their scuffles, flickering like fireflies around her ears. If she spoke, no doubt the entire building might collapse.

Baahozhonii's mother owned an art gallery. Not a sophisticated one. An art gallery that catered to jaded travelers, beckoning with the promise of a room and warm tea, tucked away from unsympathetic weather. Newcomers huddled underneath the gallery's outdoor tapestries, woven together with glaring silk—pictures of woodland creatures eaten out by moths—and counted their blessings. Patches of dark scarlet, smelling of copper, commonly stained their clothes. It rarely rained, but when it did, mud footprints trailed outside the gallery window. Strangers disrupted the soft pitter-pat of female rain with two—always two—harsh knocks.

Baahozhonii's mother owned an art gallery, and everyone called it home. She had a soft spot for the wicked and discarded. It was an art gallery full of local pieces dedicated to Baahozhonii's mother, including dead animals found alongside the road and rotting vegetables curled around peeling frames. Art, she called it. Contemporary. Novel. Fresh, she said. Baahozhonii knew desperation lined her mother's lips, raspy and wet, like spoiled lipstick. Her bangs, matted to her forehead, also dripped with sweat. It wasn't unusual, but the sight always spun her thoughts, spiderwebs caught in high ceilings.

Baahozhonii watched as her mother wiped dust off of a new piece. *I like it*, she said. *Is it his?*

The gallery accepted new work daily. Baahozhonii had never seen the Rabbit, but she knew her mother favored his art greatly.

An original. Her mother smiled.

Baahozhonii angled her head to the side. *It looks like a basket.*

It's something like that.

The Rabbit visited her mother every Friday morning. Baahozhonii was never allowed downstairs during his visits. She'd stare outside her open window, the wind freezing, biting, and cruel. Like every other stranger, he knocked twice before her mother opened the door. Baahozhonii held her breath, listening for a deep voice through the wooden floorboards. But the house creaked and groaned, seemingly on purpose. Maybe her mother bribed the interiors, the insulation, sliding promises of fresh paint or sour-juice sanding—plotting, always plotting behind her daughter's back. Baahozhonii became used to cramming frustration down her throat, only to have it pinch and creep its way back up again, drawing growls from her stomach.

In the evenings, Baahozhonii wove herself between the display cases—gliding atop mismatched socks, leaving smears in the dust. Along the walls, faces stared back at her. Portraits. Baahozhonii recognized a few of them. Their eyes were dark like her own. There were only a handful she couldn't place, eyes much too bright, starkly bright. On the very back wall, centered above the gallery's newest exhibit, was her mother. Curated with dark brush strokes beneath each eye. The right corner of her lips turned downwards.

Her portrait looked empty. Baahozhonii didn't know the artist, but she wondered if they hated her mother and painted this piece reluctantly. Her mother always complimented its depth, never once sounding disappointed or spiteful. Baahozhonii wondered if her mother saw the painting the same way she did. Hollow, fragile, and stiff.

Baahozhonii wondered.

The gallery always felt stuffy, filled to the brim, invisible hands cramming and squeezing and twisting against open space. Baahozhonii kept the windows open, begging fresh air to replace its stale counterpart. But choppy wind cascaded like tangled hair, catching uncomfortably in her mouth and ears. Another week crept by, and Baahozhonii eagerly awaited the Rabbit's arrival. When her mother talked about him, there was no quiver; gone was her mother's usual tremble. Her voice turned firm and stout. Baahozhonii wondered what it was about the Rabbit. Maybe he granted wishes, each art piece a physical representation of their bond. Maybe his eyes enchanted shopkeepers, turning them into better, temporary versions of themselves. Or maybe the Rabbit was just kind—kind enough to ease her mother's nervous falters.

At six a.m., Baahozhonii's mother chased her up the stairs. *I want to meet him*, she said.

You're too young. Her mother frowned. *He doesn't care for children.*

I help run your gallery, she cried.

You're still a child. Two short knocks interrupted them. *Quick*, she hissed. *Climb the stairs.*

Baahozhonii knew her mother was a witch. She also knew her father had been human, or at least, looked human. The next evening, while conducting her daily rounds about the gallery, Baahozhonii snuck into her mother's office. Her mother usually spent the day after the Rabbit's visit organizing a new display. He had brought another basket. It twisted and twined, like roots crisscrossing beneath the base of a large oak tree.

Her mother, preoccupied with the Rabbit's latest piece, ignored Baahozhonii. So, she snooped, digging through old boxes and tattered notebooks. Eventually she found photographs. She thought they were stolen, until Baahozhonii spotted her mother's round, youthful face.

She counted the people in the photo. One, two, three—none of them looked familiar—four, five, six—wait—seven, eight, nine, ten, eleven—here's one she recognized.

The man looked angry, maybe confused. But the shape of his face drew her in. Sharp along the sides but curved around his chin. Eyes, pools of black. But she knew, if people asked, he'd call them brown. Hair, dark and straight, falling flat against his cheeks. Skin, brown. Baahozhonii knew right away this man was her father. The human.

Baahozhonii's mother owned an art gallery. Baahozhonii hated the art gallery. Her mother never paid her any attention. Never asked her how her day went after school. Never offered to make tea in the evening. Never lulled her to sleep with a song. All Baahozhonii's mother cared about was the art gallery and the Rabbit. She acted as though they were her children, the Rabbit's pieces, cradling them, wiping their noses. It churned Baahozhonii's stomach as she watched from the corner.

Baahozhonii showed no signs of magic. Like her father, she felt very much human. She had no doubt he was dead. Magic was considered special, perhaps even sacred. A wood witch and a human together broke the rules.

Baahozhonii considered running away, but she knew no human would take her in. And no witch would recognize her as one of their own. So she stayed.

Eventually, Baahozhonii asked about the photographs. She framed her question as an accusation. *Why do I recognize him?* Tears threatened to spill from the corners of her eyes. *He shares my being. Why?* She wanted her mother to say it—to acknowledge her father, the human. Baahozhonii's mother said nothing, her features solemn and distant.

Baahozhonii thought back to the Rabbit's first visit. Her mother rushed Baahozhonii up to the attic, hastily throwing in a blanket and bread before locking the door behind her. Baahozhonii listened to her mother's footsteps scurrying down the staircase before completely disappearing. She remembered how quiet it was, her breathing seeming to echo in the empty space. Slowly, Baahozhonii wrapped the blanket around herself and sat with her back against the door. She grabbed the bread, brushing off a little bit of dust before taking a bite. From three floors above, Baahozhonii heard the knock, loud and clear. Her mother's steps returned as she opened the door.

The visitor conjured a strange air. Baahozhonii couldn't hear the visitor's voice, but her mother sounded steady, cautious. The visitor only stayed for a couple of minutes. Soon, Baahozhonii felt the attic door open behind her.

Who was that? she asked.

Baahozhonii's mother shook her head. *He's just a friend.*

The visitor had brought a sculpture. The copper material looked like branches, outlining a bare tree. Later, Baahozhonii spotted footprints. She didn't like how her mother treated them like nothing, merely sweeping the leftover dirt outside. Baahozhonii was sure a man visited, but the footprints left behind were a rabbit's.

That man, who is he? Baahozhonii didn't know if she was asking about her father or about the Rabbit. But she didn't have time to ponder it. Swiftly, her mother struck her across the face. Baahozhonii noticed the scars along her mother's neck, the fear that laced her irises.

Don't speak nonsense, her mother said. *You sound like your father.*

Baahozhonii realized she'd never find out who that man was.

Baahozhonii's mother owned an art gallery. Not a fancy one. An art gallery that smelled like bare neglect and lost love. It stole identities and demanded entrance into dreams. An art gallery that catered to everyone's worst self, a step away from morality and a turn toward distrust. Tread carefully, it said, and remember to check your pockets. Expect to be confronted, not by a person, but by cruel judgment.

Not a tasteful one; an art gallery full of discarded musings. Filled to the brim with rotten tomatoes, boxes full of old books, and jars listing essential oils. Frayed paintings, depicting faintly smug smiles; the corner of their mouths upturned. Baahozhonii knew they were mocking her from a time beyond her own.

She would never know their secrets, and the people in the paintings took too much pleasure in her frustration. If she closed her eyes, Baahozhonii could hear their whispers, like ants along the wall. And if she took a deep breath, Baahozhonii could smell wet fur.

Danielle Shandiin Emerson is a Diné writer from Shiprock, on the Navajo Nation. Her clans are Tłaashchi'i (Red Cheek People Clan), *born for Ta'neezaahnii* (Tangled People Clan). *Her maternal grandfather is Ashįįhí (Salt People Clan) and her paternal grandfather is Táchii'nii (Red Running into the Water People Clan). She has a B.A. in Education Studies and a B.A. in Literary Arts from Brown University.*

Green Chile Stew

Harper O'Connor

We are not
A melting pot.
We do not blend
into a single amalgamation, a mixed alloy
To be poured into a mold
And popped out
Once cold.
We are green chile stew
Simmered for hours and hotter the next day–
We are pieces in your mouth.
He is the chunks of fatty pork melting
On your tongue.
She is the tomato, hot and bursting softness, the red of summer;
I am the onion (or maybe the garlic), diced
And translucent con Sazón.
They are the chiles: maybe Hatch, maybe

Jalapeño,
Maybe Anaheim or Poblano,
All green and grown here with their skin blackened
By your gas stove's burner, air thickened with their roasting aroma.
We are bites full of textures
Dripping in layers
Con mucho sabores.

Harper O'Connor is a nonbinary disabled quirky Albuquerque-based writer owned by one or more cats. Their inspirations range from Stephen King to Audre Lorde and they draw on a complex and occasionally traumatic multinational past. Off the page, they are a passionate crafter in ink and textiles.

Her Whole Life a Turtle

Margaret Grayson

irstly, it should be established that we do not endorse the kidnapping of tortoises. If a tortoise is found crawling across the highway in the Mojave Desert, one should not, under any circumstances, put said tortoise in the back of the station wagon and drive her to the California coast, congratulating oneself along the way for having performed a valiant rescue. But alas, this was the very choice made by some of my relatives, cousins of my mother's family, who have remained anonymous in the retellings of their crime. They brought a tortoise to Santa Maria and gave her to my grandparents, where she became both pet and family heirloom.

Decades later, desert tortoises were listed as threatened and it became extra illegal to take them from the wild. My grandparents got in touch with a wildlife official to see if they ought to put her back, but the expert thought she would be both incapable of fending for herself and a disease liability for her fellow tortoises. And so my family was grandfathered into possession of an illegal tortoise.

In defense of the cousins, it was 1969, a year of moon landings and war protests and Manson family murders and Creedence Clearwater Revival. I'm willing to acquiesce that there were likely more-pressing concerns on their minds than the ecological conservation of tortoises, though the tortoises were already quietly marching toward decline. This is the whole trouble with tortoises, actually; you set a tortoise on the front lawn and think that you're free to look away for a few moments and then you lose track of the moments and look back and the tortoise is not where you left her. If a tortoise gets it in her head to go somewhere she will heave her shell off the ground and go and not stop for anything.

The very same tortoise kidnapped in California would end up lost in Colorado more than once, and every time, panic ensued. You can judge a person's crisis-response facility in such situations; every minute you spend crying over the lost tortoise, the search radius expands by roughly six inches in all directions, which is not nothing. Once we searched for an hour and found her a few hundred yards away from the house, tunneling through pasture grasses, headed west, maybe toward the irrigation ditch or maybe toward California.

My mother's family acquired the tortoise when my mother was six, and they counted the rings on the tortoise's shell and determined her to also be six. Her name was Timothy and her gender was subject to debate. Physically, all signs pointed to her being a female tortoise. (Tortoise penises are reportedly quite horrifying; "If you had a male, you'd *know*," said someone familiar with such things.) But once, she was put in proximity to a male tortoise and she tried to fight him, which was my grandmother's lifelong evidence for Timothy being a boy, though I purport she was merely a feminist. So my immediate family called Timothy "she" and my grandparents called Timothy "he" and in the end it didn't matter at all. How very progressive. We did insist on correcting anyone who called her a turtle.

Timothy grew to be about the size of a basketball. My father built her a pen off the back porch, and within the pen a smaller brick pen enclosure with a makeshift roof. We fed her dandelion greens and purslane and daylily leaves and put out shallow trays of water in which she would dunk her chin and blow bubbles. If we moved slowly enough we could stroke the top of her head with a finger. Around Thanksgiving we'd put her in a box in the basement and leave her there until the dandelions bloomed in the spring. She slept through every winter, not eating or drinking, until her very last year alive, during which she was inexplicably restless.

There are advantages to being slow and sleepy and durable. A desert tortoise can wait out hot dry spells and sleep through long freezing nights, hide its soft limbs away from predators and urinate as a defense mechanism; if the tortoises survive adolescence, as only a small percentage do, they may live to be 50-80 years old. One thing a tortoise cannot withstand is upside-downedness, which is why the primary objective of brawling male tortoises is toppling and why my sister and I were sent outside to check on Timothy every few days, lest she try to climb too high, lose her balance and find herself in such an awkward position.

Another thing the tortoises find difficult is habitat loss. Ideally, a tortoise would have up to 40 acres to wander without having to worry about highways or inedible invasive grasses eating up desert landscapes or disagreeable neighbor tortoises or yahoos on off-road vehicles. Along with human development come enterprising ravens, trailing just behind and eagerly dining on whatever new food source we churn up in our wake. The ravens have developed a taste for young tortoise, leaving some conservationists trying creative methods to deter the birds, using lasers and 3D-printing hyper-realistic booby-trapped fake tortoise shells to scare the predator when it leans in to peck.

Despite all this, and despite the fact that she lived her later years many hundreds of miles from her preferred habitat, my family had to do very little to keep Timothy alive. We joked that she'd outlive all of us and be handed down through generations like family china. But she died quietly and without known cause in the summer of 2022 and my dad buried her in the woods near the other pets who'd come and gone in the intervening years. She was at least 60 years old.

Months later my dad and I were listening to a podcast episode on turtles, and we were both annoyed when the host mentioned tortoises. "There's a difference," we said to each other self-righteously. We had a friend who was a tortoise, so obviously we knew. But then the podcast host explained that tortoises are just a type of turtle. We had been, for years, correcting people for no reason, and Timothy had been her whole life a turtle, and we had not known.

It was like that. Half a century in and there was still no consensus on the basic biological fact of her sex. We did not read books on tortoise care or take her to the veterinarian. We kept her more the way you keep a tree than the way you keep a dog. We took her for granted, except for those few occasions when she was lost, when suddenly the whole world rested on the back of a turtle.

Our knowledge of Timothy was based on observation, including observation that had been handed down rather than personally observed. My mom and her siblings had all, at some point, experimented with sticking their fingers in her mouth while she was eating, and had been surprised at the force of her blunt, toothless jaw, and then too embarrassed to admit to having done it until years later. I grew up hearing this story, and so my sister and I never got anywhere close to her chewing, and when friends asked, "Does she bite?" I would say, "Only if you put your finger in her mouth," and everyone would chuckle with relief.

One day when I was a teenager I slid into my flip-flops and flopped out the back door to the tortoise pen to bring Timothy food and water. She was awake and alert, and she took notice of my arrival in a way that was unusual—often it felt like human presence was utterly incidental to her so long as we didn't move too quickly. But I sat on the low brick wall of her enclosure and watched her gaze focus intensely on my feet.

Her consciousness was a mystery to me. What spurred her to move when she did, or to stay still at every other moment? What was she thinking and feeling? Did she mind being a pet, or think it strange that her food was delivered in a damp pile before her instead of sought among the dry eaves of the desert? It was fascinating to watch her move once she put her mind to it. I could see the machinery working like a wind-up toy, see the gears and pulleys that lifted each scaled foot and pulled it forward, see the care that each step required. It was movement deconstructed. She walked toward me like a puddle of water seeping across the ground, slow and inevitable. I watched her stretch her neck out, a flex of skin and vein and muscle, all dinosaur. She was still looking at my feet, my shiny blue-polished toenails, and we looked at them together and I wondered for the first time if she could see color, and if so, which colors.

She reached for me, winching open her jaw, her mouth opening at roughly the rate that the North American continent is drifting away from the Eurasian continent. All at once I came to and very quickly pulled my foot away, having been so wrapped up in her primordial strangeness, so busy mythologizing all that was unknowable and incommunicable about her, that I had not recognized her simple and obvious intention, which was to bite my toe.

Margaret Grayson is an essayist and journalist from southwest Colorado. She has an MFA in creative writing from Washington University in St. Louis, qualifying her to hold several part-time customer service jobs at once. She loves to run, make pottery, talk about her dog and lose at cribbage.

Breakfast on the Fall Equinox

Brandi Blaisdell

It's my butter,
no one else to share it
so why does it matter
what utensil I use,
the oatmeal-contaminated knife
or just-licked spoon?

In some ways,
it's like living alone
since my husband's Crohn's diagnosis.
Some meals go unshared.
Dinners more like science experiments,
developing a thesis on safe food combinations.

My diagnosis is loneliness.
Experts say it's like smoking

fifteen cigarettes a day.
Is that literal or figurative?
Either way, they imply
I'm doing it to myself.
Why don't I just look cool and aloof?
Where is my box of patches or gum?

I eat my buttery oatmeal alone.
The sun rises slowly these fall days.

Brandi Blaisdell is a gardener, poet, and photographer living in Southwestern Colorado. Brandi's poems have been published in "3 Panel Poetry" and "Word Honey" zines and exhibited in the interactive multimedia art collaboration "Voices Inside My Head" and "Voices Inside My Head: Echo."

Digger

David Feela

1.

In the fall, when the gods turn off the water, shortly after the cottonwood leaves start sputtering like candle flames, Digger exhumes his hiking boots from the back of his closet where he parks them all spring and all summer. An old layer of mud crumbles to the floor as he lifts them toward the light. The sound of sand breaking loose from his boots reminds him of his old Etch-A-Sketch when he turns it upside down to shake the screen clean.

As he crisscrosses the laces and cinches up the tension, Digger marvels that the boots still fit his feet. He grows like a cattail, his mother claims, everything but his feet, which suits him. He loves his boots as much as he loves his feet. He sees no reason for a new pair of either.

"Digger, don't you put those boots on in this house!"

"How am I supposed to get to the door?"

"I don't care, walk on your hands, but those boots better not touch the floor."

"How am I supposed to carry my boots if I walk on my hands?"

"You're a smart boy, you'll think of something."

Digger sits on the floor in front of his closet and thinks very hard about taking off his boots until his bedroom window begins to glow with the early morning sunlight.

Not even the house hears him leave.

2.

Digger is Doug, or rather, Doug is Digger—Douglas, to be precise—named after his great-grandfather, an archaeologist who worked in the American Southwest. Digger's father, before he died in a freak accident involving the hydraulic crusher on the back of one of his company's garbage trucks, was a part of the family in Moline, Illinois. After the funeral, mother and son moved back to her roots in Southwestern Colorado.

The boy, even at the age of ten, resembles his great-grandfather, with a prominent nose, wide shoulders supporting shoulder blades that jut out like the stumps of wings on his back, and those robin's egg blue eyes. His fingers are too long, he thinks, like the tines on his mom's gardening rake, which is why he constantly shoves them into his pockets when other people are around.

Nothing about his new home disappoints him. The dry mountain air relieves the humidity of the Midwest, and the sky opens like a promise nearly every morning. Even his nickname fell from the sky, almost as if it were birdsong, when his grandpa whistled for his attention.

"Go ahead, just ignore the grandpa who drove an hour to come see you."

"I didn't ignore you. You snuck up on me."

"Ha! I caught you dancing with that shovel."

"Shovels don't dance, they dig."

"Diggers dig, shovels hum the melody."

"I don't hear nothing."

"You'll never hear anything if you keep talking when you're supposed to listen."

3.

The rusted steel gate squeals its aria as Digger opens and closes it, dutifully hooking the chain. He usually scales it like a ladder and vaults over the top, but today he courts the properness of things. He brushes the bangs of his sandy-blonde hair away from his forehead and glances along the ditch bank in both directions, then sets off at a brisk pace downstream.

The rutted road, the width of a pickup truck, runs for miles along an irrigation canal, every mile or so interrupted by an access gate, chained and locked at the end of each irrigation season. He scales them easily. After the irrigation water has been off and if the weather stays dry enough, a jigsaw puzzle of interlocking puddles begins to evaporate and the mud at the bottom of the canal firms up. He'll walk on it, eventually, down there along the path where the water usually runs, where no gates stand in his way. He kicks at every scrap of debris he finds sticking up from the clay bottom with the toe of a boot, hoping to unearth another lost thing.

But to keep everything he finds would be impossible. The box in his closet contains a few screwdrivers, pliers, and wrenches, one corroded pocketknife, blued glass bottles, and wild-haired paintbrushes. Coins too. He'd found a silver dollar once, and a plastic credit card deposited in the silt from upstream.

Digger also finds bones, more often than he cares to, mostly skeletal parts: ribs, hooves, and skulls. Jaws and teeth. Never a human corpse, though sometimes he wonders. Almost always the water scrubs them clean, so picking them up for a closer look doesn't make him squeamish. Once he'd carried home the perfectly intact skeleton of a mouse. How all those tiny white bones stayed together in the rush of current remains a mystery, one he saves but doesn't care to solve.

Today, because so much of the canal bed is still muddy, he decides to stay dry and survey from the bank for a few more days. When he spots a promising dimple in the mud, he makes a tiny stack of stones to mark where he might later dig. Digger marvels at the many animal tracks pocked like dotted lines into the mud, descending, no doubt, to drink from the few remaining puddles that reflect the sunlight, glittering like primal jewels.

No living creature ever comes to the canal without taking something away.

4.

"Don't you have homework to finish?"

"I did it at school."

"Show me."
"I didn't bring it home!"
"This is the third day you did your homework at school."
"That's because it's schoolwork, not homework."
"I want to see what you're learning at school."
"I'm not learning nothing."
"You can say that again."
"I'm not learning nothing."
"Anything."
"So you'll let me do anything?"

"I mean you should say anything, not nothing."

"What's wrong with nothing."

"Nothing, except when you say it."

"Can I go?"

"May I go."

"Mothers don't need to ask permission."

5.

A philosophy of lost things has never been written, or if it has, it was lost. Digger accepts that much of what he uncovers is merely discarded, and what better repository for abandonment than hitching it to a moving thread of water, to be tugged out of sight? He's watched ranchers and teenagers toss old tires off a bridge rather than drive the extra half mile to the county landfill. He's seen plastic bags chucked over the edge, believing they were just trash until one missed the water and struck the bank, splitting open and spilling a half-dozen kittens like a mound of writhing worms.

A philosophy of lost things contains sorrow. It should be written on pages the thickness of tissue. Digger knew nothing about loss until his father died, until the people around him told him how devastated he must be feeling. But he only felt numb, never having known the man who married his mother. On the rare occasion when his father stayed home, the hours hung like wet laundry. Terrible as it sounds, when he was gone, a breeze lifted Digger's spirits until his mother softly folded her son and put him to bed.

The box in Digger's closet does not contain souvenirs. It holds objects that when he'd first pulled them loose from the damp clay, he knew they'd been missed. How does a boy tell his mother—tell anyone, really—why he tosses out an old spoon but treasures a soggy baseball? To say the one holds a glimmer of light and the other doesn't amounts to explaining the inexplicable. Once his mother had asked, sitting down beside the sink while Digger scrubbed the mud from an old cowboy spur with a toothbrush, letting her elbows rest on the counter, the unfathomable question.

"Why do you need these things?"

"I don't know."

"Digger, I don't care, but try to tell me why."

He let the water run into the sink, the stream of it hissing like a whisper, pummeling the spur until it was finally submerged. Then he pulled the plug, and they both listened while the vortex sucked all the loose dirt out of sight. His mother still waited, elbows propped, her chin resting in the nest of her fingers, watching him. Digger picked up the spur and patted it dry with a ragged towel that hung from his belt, then lifted it to inspect it against the 60-watt bulb burning above the sink.

"I don't know. Maybe it reminds me of something I forgot."

"Well then, at least that's something."

6.

When Digger stays out until sunset, or later, his mother worries. Each time she hears the steel gate squeal she jumps up, then quickly sits back down, doing her best to moderate her uneasiness. Bury it like a bone. Never let fear find its way home.

Once she'd asked Digger if he'd like a dog. The boy answered immediately, without a moment of consideration. No, he didn't want the competition. So it surprises her when he bursts into the house breathless, shouting for her audience, as if she isn't sitting right in front of him in her evening reading chair with the lamplight bright on her face.

"Mom, guess what I found!"

"A gold nugget? We could use one of those."

"No, just listen."

She sets her book aside, patting the seat beside her.

"Can't sit."

"Well then, you'll just have to talk."

"Can't talk, not hardly. Been running at least a mile."

"Why have you been running?"

"Being chased."

"Chased?"

She stands up from her chair and moves toward Digger, maybe to help him out of his coat, or to wrap him in her arms. She isn't sure. Either way, Digger backs up, matching the distance she moves forward, like magnets with the wrong poles fixed on each other. She is about to ask who or what was chasing him when she sees the pig through the open doorway. A large pig, attired in mud. A hundred pounds of pig, maybe more. A pig staring quizzically into her sitting room.

As Digger turns toward the yard, her arm strikes like a rattler, nabbing Digger by his jacket sleeve and pulling him into the house, slamming and locking the door with her other hand, all in one fluid, maternal motion.

"Mom, it's just a pig."

"Is that what chased you home?"

"Only part ways. Then he followed me."

"He? That pig doesn't look too friendly."

"You haven't spent any time with him."

"I don't want to. Do you?"

"He likes digging in the mud at the bottom of the canal. That's where I found him."

"Just like you."

"It's not the same thing. He uses his nose."

"Did you throw rocks? Is that why he chased you?"

"No, I grabbed a boot he uncovered after I thought he'd moved on."

"What boot?"

"It's back in the canal where I tossed it. That's what he was after, not me."

"So why is the pig still outside our door?"

"I don't know."

"Did you feed it?"

"He grabbed my apple when it fell out of my pocket. I didn't tell him he could eat it."

"Well then, you're even. Let's all call it a day."

Closing the blinds and shutting off the lights, Digger's mother nudges him through the darkened sitting room and toward his bed-room.

"Mom, I think that pig is lonely."

"That pig is hungry. It's not the same."

"Are we gonna leave him out there?"

"By morning he'll wander back to the place where he lives. Good-night, Digger."

Pausing beside his bedroom door, his mother sees the confusion brewing on Digger's face. She gives him a kiss on the forehead, hoping it says without saying, don't worry.

"What if he's still here in the morning?"

"We'll ask if he wants bacon and eggs for breakfast."

7.

Digger swallows his breakfast as if he's inhaling the morning air. Before his hand reaches for his gathering bag on the chair beside him, his mother touches his shoulder.

"Back before sunset?"

"Yes."

"Do you need a lunch?"

"I need to hurry."

"Why?"

"I'm late."

"But it's early."

"I gotta go."

"Your lunch is already packed."

"Okay."

"Peanut butter and this time two apples."

"Thanks, mom."

After circling the house twice, then once to the end of the driveway for a look in both directions along the county road, Digger realizes his mother must be right, that every lost thing has a home.

The gate squeals its usual hello and goodbye as Digger heads for the ditch, his bag over his shoulder, his digging tool dangling from his carpenter's belt.

He'd found the belt hanging from a water release valve, wide as his mother's steering wheel. Immediately he was tempted to take the belt home. But he left it there, watching it in the sun and rain for two full weeks, like waiting to open a present under a Christmas tree. Not only would his prospector's hammer fit securely in the belt's clasp, but it contained pouches where the tiniest of things could be safely stowed.

A few strides from the gate, Digger stops. His brain eavesdrops on his ears and whispers that something is wrong, that the gate is still squealing, as if someone is standing there repeatedly pushing it open and yanking it closed. He looks back toward the house. Nobody. He marches a dozen more paces. Stops. Listens.

Nothing. But as he turns away he hears the sound, continuous now, as if the cold steel gate has transformed into an animate being. A squeal made of cold rust becoming a hot-blooded thing.

Digger rushes back to unchain the gate, to confront his fear. But it's no imaginary beast. It's the pig. It's miraculously the pig that followed him home and now seems to be insisting on following him again. One of the apples in his pocket bumps against his hand. He's tempted to pull it out and toss it on the ground between them but he hears his mother's admonition in his head against baiting the desires of his heart. If they come of their own volition, then he has earned the right to decide what stays lost and what wants finding. He faces the ditch and hurries along. Pig trots after him.

8.

Digger usually hikes along the irrigation canal for over an hour, but today he spots a mound halfway down the embankment only ten minutes from home, where an animal appears to have been burrowing a tunnel. Wild things don't care what they uncover. They push obstacles out of the way or work around them like he does with his fork when his mother tries to sneak mushrooms onto his dinner plate. He grabs a sturdy stick from along the fence for prodding the tunnel's depth, for defending himself if need be against what may be inside, defending itself. Once such a hissing erupted from inside a hole that he thought the sound would burn like the steam from his father's broken radiator hose. Even then, Digger knew enough to back away. Claws and teeth don't wait for explanations.

During Digger's hike, pig plods along at the bottom of the canal where the dirt remains moist, sniffing and investigating, not keeping up, then squealing and running faster than Digger ever expected a pig to move. Like a dog, pig is easily distracted, but Digger is pleased to see pig almost keeping up. He smiles. He's taking pig for a trot.

Carefully descending the crumbling bank, Digger kicks footholds into the dirt, eventually one foot on each side of the mound's entrance so he won't slip further toward the muddy bottom. He steadies himself with the stick, wishing he'd brought a flashlight as he bends to peer inside. Immediately Digger hears a fierce grunting and winded breathing. The dirt collapses under his boots. He slides the full length of his body down the embankment before his feet catch a new purchase in the loose soil. Glancing down, Digger sees the ruckus is just pig scrambling from below, upsetting his balance, straight past him, up toward the mound's opening.

All Digger can do is watch, and wait, while pig destroys the tunnel's entrance as if competing with Digger for the first peek. Pig digs, his butt and back legs wiggling, the dislodged dirt trickling down on him like sand from an hourglass until pig dislodges a clod of dirt as large as a skull, rolling toward Digger. Before it crashes into him, Digger raises his head and traps it beneath his body, the clod becoming his new center of gravity.

"Knock it off!" Digger shouts.

To his amazement, pig backs out of the crater he carved, climbs to the road, sits, and stares back down, eyes shining like precious pink garnets. Suddenly the clod sheltered by Digger's body starts to crumble under his weight. Loose sand slips away as he feels the lump disintegrating. But no, something solid stays, something at its core. With one hand he reaches for it and slips what remains into his gathering bag, then climbs like a spider up to the solid road.

David Feela has published three books of poetry. His earlier essay collection, How Delicate These Arches *(Raven's Eye Press, 2011), was a finalist for the Colorado Book Award.* Feelasophy: Selected Essays, *is his second. He lives in Cortez. Visit davidfeela.com to view his website.*

Whistle

Burton E. Baldwin

As a boy he read Will James.
He used to say that memory
was a kind of silence,
and that seeking fortunes
was the straightest path to hell.
He warned me
that when I got older,
and if I wasn't wary,
I could end up shipwrecked
on the prairie of my dreams.
I can still hear
the quick whistle
as his remuda swam
through the salt brush and sage,
down the slope,
gaining momentum,

a slow thunderous cloud.
They headed south like some flotilla,
into the arroyo, creating
a dusty swirl.
I could barely see him,
hands folded over the horn,
rocking in the saddle
like some old sea captain,
the brim pushed up and bent,
his unique signature;
and again, that sharp whistle,
through the dust devil,
and "Ole Socks" the heeler responding.
Sweat trailed sinew,
they slowly faded
over the edge of the day
and into the shadows
of another time.

Burton E. Baldwin is an educator and writer. He has published three volumes of poetry and one of Young Adult Fiction. His poetry and essays have appeared regularly for the past 25 years in the Durango Telegraph, Four Corners Free Press, *and Colorado Country Life.*

The Land of the Giants

Paddy Keelan

Grand Canyon
River Mile 74.8

Boats have been mostly rigged, sunscreen is being slath-
ered on limbs, a toothbrush or two are poking out of mouths. A pair
of uncovered tits in the breeze.

"You guys ready for a brief?"

I think back to flying in Afghanistan, and our pre-departure
"briefs." Anything but. Hours long. Way beyond the time limit of
useful consciousness. I aim to be concise, yet cover some important
shit.

"Okay, guys, first up is Hance Rapid, absolutely one of the big-
gest and most difficult of the entire trip. We will pull over on river
right to scout it. The entry is key; you want to be stern first ferrying
hard left, and try to tuck into a piece of disturbed water behind the
big boulder at the top. It's called the duck pond. There is a bare-
ly-submerged guard rock that you should try to miss as you enter,

or it could fuck up your line really quick. Watch that downstream oar! The most important thing is to keep working left. Never stop working left. River right is full of massive waves and holes and rocks, and it's called The Land of the Giants. You do not want to be there. In fact, it's one of the worst places to find yourself between Lee's and Diamond Creek."

Just then, something from the sky slams into the sand at my feet. I scan the faces of the circle around me to find the guilty party. All appear equally confused.

I bend down and pick up the pink gummy eraser at my feet. Hear a taunting "CAW CAW!!" above and spy two jet-black forms winging their way upriver.

One of them must have swooped down nearby, spying a tasty piece of Spam from above. What utter fucking disappointment!

I'm not sure if it was pure chance that it landed at my feet or if the ravens are just that dialed in their bombing runs. Voicing their displeasure at human deceit and trickery. Either way, it gives me pause, and though I'm not prone to omens or horoscopes or planetary alignments or Mercury-in-retrograde signs of superstition, this seems extra weird.

Is Hance about to erase me?

On my first Grand trip in 2017, Hance was hands-down my worst run. I was so tunnel-focused on making the duck pond that I missed the snake-in-the-grass guard rock. And by missed, I mean hit. Slammed right into the fucker, popped my downstream oar out of the lock immediately. The rest of the rapid was an assholes-and-elbows attempt at trying to square up to big waves while wrestling the oar back into its lock. We somehow emerged upright, soaked and mewing. Somehow missed The Land of the Giants. The one-armed man got lucky. I don't intend to test the patience of the river gods again.

Or is the eraser telling me that I may replace that nightmare with a good run this time?

I'm not sure which oracle to consult, and I'm not willing to swan-dive into the gobbledygook just yet. But I do slip the eraser into my pocket. Leave no trace.

Leave no trace of me?

We head back to the boats. John is inhaling cigarettes at the tie-up. I don't think I've seen someone burn one down so fast in my life. I pat him on the shoulder and force a smile as I coil my bowline. Push off. Yell back to shore: "Have a great run, guys!"

As you accelerate into a rapid, your group quickly recedes behind you. In a long, complex rapid like Hance, it will be all but impossible to keep track of the group until we all emerge out the other side of the wormhole at the end, something like a half-mile downstream. There will barely be any time to regroup before the boats are swept into Son of Hance, just immediately after. Each boat is an island unto itself.

I am laser-focused on nailing my entry, trying to demonstrate a good line to those who will follow, particularly the three Grand Canyon virgin boatmen.

Though we just kiss the guard rock, I see it coming and time my strokes to not repeat mistakes of the past, pulling hard into the duck pond. The current differential spins my bow, and from there it's a big ride of waves, occasionally ferrying left or slightly right as I work left through the problem. The run goes great, and I'm high on adrenaline as we ride out the tail waves. I have no idea what is occurring a half-mile above me.

I pull upstream to slow down and let the group catch up, but I can't stop my boat from being swept down into Son of Hance. Quickly back into the shit, squaring up and finally finding an eddy at the bottom of Son to pause and regroup.

The other boats slowly make their way to my eddy. One. Two. Three. Four. At last, Five. Everyone is upright, hooting and hollering, and stoked to have passed through the gauntlet. One thing appears out of sorts on one boat, but I can't yet place it.

Ah yes. Why is Justin rowing John's boat?

I hear the harrowing tale.

Just after John finished sucking down cigarettes like an SR-71 pilot pre-breathing oxygen before a high-altitude mission on the black edge of space, it all fell apart.

Despite my emphasizing the hidden guard rock in hopes of sparing boatmen my fate in '17, John was so amped up that he forgot all about it. While he was standing up to get a better view of the chaos ahead, his boat slammed into the sneaky bastard and John plopped, ass over teacups, out of his own boat and into the rio.

"Save yourselves!" he yelled to his passengers, Erica and her boyfriend Justin, as he was swept away into the Giants.

My good friend Justin, despite never having rowed a boat in his life, is cool under pressure. We flew together in Afghanistan and he's saved my life twice. Having watched us maneuvering boats for a week, and possessing an aviator's native understanding of differential thrust, Justin immediately hopped into the cockpit and began his rowing career in one of the most difficult rapids in Grand Canyon. After safely navigating himself and his lady down the turbulent waters, he tracked down and rescued his own boatman, a very wet and very humbled John.

All of this was accomplished before the rendezvous in the eddy below Son of Hance, and I was none the wiser. A large part of me is glad I didn't even see it, because as a TL you feel the same protective urges of a mother duck, trying to keep the whole party safely together. I had failed my crew.

John had swum the Giants. And by swum, I mean that he had periodically lucked out enough to pop up to the surface for a quick breath before the next massive, chundering hole swallowed him down again into what surely must have seemed like an eternal spin cycle. Hydraulic after hydraulic had grabbed him and pulled him under, the river gods screaming, "Fuck you!" again and again and again.

Somehow John had missed colliding with any of the boulders lurking below the surface, and thanks to Justin's lightning-fast reactions and penchant for being an all-around quick study, John was now seated back in his boat after the ride, sucking down another cancer stick, trying to process what the fuck just happened and how he had lived through it.

After hearing the tale firsthand, the nurses in our group do a quick assessment on John. He's clearly shaken up but physically just fine. And furthermore, he is now officially a member of the Grand Canyon Swim Team! We continue downstream, while Mike, one of my other veteran boatmen, gleefully informs the flotilla about the bootie beer coming up in camp tonight.

"What's a bootie beer?" John asks.

"We shake and pour a warm shitty lager into someone's stinky neoprene boot, and then you have to chug it," Mike responds.

"Yeah, I'm not doing that."

"It's not optional. If you swim, you have to do it. It's river tradition, back to Powell's day, and traditions will be upheld."

"I'm not doing it."

"Okay, whatever. We'll hold you down and waterboard you if we have to."

Later that afternoon, after a smooth run by all through Sockdolager, we decide to camp at the wonderful beach at Grapevine. It's the last night for two of our crew before the exchange at Phantom. Mike and Richard will be hiking out, and my friends Rob, Nate, and my sister Kellie will be hiking in for the second part of the trip. We party hard, celebrating our survival of Hance and our last night with two of our tribe.

John begrudgingly yields to traditions, and is served a warm, slightly shaken Rainier in Emma's boot by a grinning, American-flag-Speedo-clad Mike.

At the golden hour, I stand alone on a high point overlooking Grapevine beach and listen to the musical laughter and canyon bliss echoing off walls and mixing with the soft gurgling of moving waters.

The river continues to rush by.

Paddy Keelan lives with his wife, young daughter, dog, and cat in the aspens outside Durango. He gets out on the water as often as possible. This excerpt is from a forthcoming book about Grand Canyon and his life as a bush pilot in three separate war zones.

Vision Quest on Highway 550

Claire Crabtree

I met my other on a mountain steepness,
In a rental car, the headlights of others
Thinning as we climbed,
The airbag's wallop and no sight
But a knowing and shaking—
A strange stopping of car and beast.

The trooper wrote what I said, the truth:
I saw nothing until after.
But the windshield was cracked:
A gray bear shape perhaps, rolled up and off,
And yes, it had come from the left.

They came for us, my son and his girl—
Trucks and menfolk all around
Doing the right and careful things.

She chanted as I shook beside the road,
This was not my doing, this meeting:
He chose to meet me.

Not then, not in waking, did I remember
The thick-legged shape not loping but running
Mountain to meadow
In the exigency before Winter,
And his sad halting,
Whose fur, as we knelt in grief
At the edge of a Colorado highway
Where the men had dragged him for safety,
Felt so startling, so kindly, so soft.

Claire Crabtree, a Durango resident, has served as a professor of English in Michigan, publishing literary criticism as well as poetry. Her poems have appeared in many publications, including America, So to Speak Journal, Phoebe Journal, Passages North, *and* Earth's Daughters, *in which "Vision Quest on Highway 550" appeared in 2016.*

Western Awakening

Otis Kunz

Jersey City, in the 1950s and '60s, was the opposite of rural America. No corn fields, Grange halls, square dances, or hayrides. In the years after World War II, there was the occasional tomato garden, lovingly tended by an old Italian granddad. Straw hat, white shirt, black pants held up by suspenders, harvesting the ripe fruit for his wife to put up for sauce. Tomatoes zealously guarded from the neighborhood kids who treated his produce as ammunition for a firefight. In the evenings, he and his paisans would sit under the grape arbor, sip last year's homemade wine, and reminisce about the old country.

The police department still had a stable for its mounted patrol, later converted into a motorcycle garage. Horses swapped for Harleys. Victory gardens paved over for parking. From a rooftop coop, a man waving a long bamboo pole with a white flag, flying his flock of homing pigeons. An immigrant family might have a couple of hens in the backyard. That was pretty much it for critters, if you didn't count the rats.

Jersey City was not, however, all concrete. Bracketed by the Holland Tunnel on the south side and the Lincoln Tunnel to the north, it was fronted by docks from a bygone era, all falling into disrepair. The local kids built up their immune systems by jumping into the Hudson River, multicolored with oil slicks and God knows what else in those days.

Pete Seeger and the Riverkeepers had yet to appear on scene, and so the Hudson was still a dumping ground along its fetid length. Older, retired factory workers sat on the rickety piers, fishing poles in hand, or threw crab traps on long ropes into the murky depths. Not that anyone would eat anything from that river. It was just something to do.

The western shore of the Hudson was where rural New Jersey started. The frontier for city kids. Freight trains constantly rumbled through, headed to and from the greater metropolis of New York City. They were often slow enough for the more adventurous kids to grab a boxcar ladder and hitch a ride. Sometimes a freight car door was open, and they'd hop in and head out to the open space of the Meadows, hoping it would eventually slow down enough to allow them to jump off and catch a different freight back. Living out a hobo fantasy, hoping the railroad bulls wouldn't spot them and fill their asses with the rock salt with which they kept their shotgun shells loaded.

To the east lay lower Manhattan. A short train ride led to Greenwich Village, where, as a Dylan song would later announce, there was "music and revolution in the air." A little longer on the train would take you to Grand Central, a portal to and from anywhere in America. A few minutes' walk from there brought you to the sleazy insanity of 42nd Street and Times Square, with its peep shows, pimps, and hustlers on every block.

The mindset of most folks growing up in Jersey City was that success was a bite of the Big Apple. Which is why the trains from the Jersey side were full heading into Manhattan from 6:15 in the morning to around 10 with commuters heading into their 9-to-5s. Then the trains would backfill from 5 p.m. onward, heading home. Have some supper, a little TV time. Put the kids to bed and turn around and do it again tomorrow.

Vacation time was either "down the Shore" for a week, where you could rent a couple of rooms and squeeze your family into a tiny kitchenette to cook dinner and slather Noxzema onto the sunburn, or else "up the mountains" to the Poconos or the Borscht Belt of the Catskills, depending on your ethnicity.

Once every few years the family could afford to pile into the car and head to Florida. For city people, driving to Florida was a high adventure of two-lane highways through tiny towns and hamlets, trying to avoid the speed traps and stopping at Stuckey's for breakfast after staying in the roadside motor courts, the kids filling up on waffles and syrup. These were the days when you might come across a chain gang working on the verge, and where some diners and town-square water fountains still had "White Only" signs. Disney World hadn't yet been conceived, let alone built, so the family entertainment was confined to the ocean, or to watching the Seminoles wrestle alligators at the roadside petting zoos.

Jack Chapman loved that drive as a kid. Something about the open road always called to him. He was just old enough to obtain his driver's license, and he'd just started dating Liz, who'd already graduated from a Catholic high school and was working as a secretary in New York. Jack still had a few months of make-up work to do before graduating from his public high school. He was behind, thanks to Greenwich Village being a little too close and a little too easy to access.

He and Liz had already started talking about life after school. Liz, mostly, had ideas of how life should be planned out, based on the role models of their parents. The previous generation had lived through and come home from WWII, didn't talk about it much, and went to work building a better life for their kids.

With that generation as an example and influence, life was laid out on a fairly straight path. Finish school, sow a few wild oats, settle down, start a career, get married, and raise some kids. Rinse and repeat. But LBJ and Robert McNamara had other ideas, and life was about to turn out differently than expected for an entire generation.

Jack Chapman was drafted.

Liz, joined by Jack's family and friends, had escorted him to the bus station when he was due to report to Ft. Dix. They waved him off with tearful promises to write frequently, stay faithful, and wait for his return. There was no one there to meet him as he got off the bus, unrecognizable, three years later. As he walked, still in uniform, to his parents' house, no one on the streets said hello as he passed. Most looked away, or else stared in thinly veiled scorn. The streets of his hometown seemed strangely unfamiliar. There was more traffic than he'd remembered, and long-haired kids hung out on his old street corners.

As he turned into the block where he'd grown up, he saw his dad on the porch painting the trim. His mom was sitting on the stoop with a book on her lap. They both glanced his way, but Jack had lost thirty pounds and stood an inch or two taller. It wasn't until he'd stopped on the sidewalk that they'd realized their son was home.

His mom's book fell to the curb as she shrieked, bounded up, and hugged him painfully hard as if she'd never let him go. His father, upon seeing the two Purple Hearts and a Bronze Star among the campaign ribbons on Jack's chest, looked Jack in the eye, gripped his hand, and said in a quavering voice, "Welcome home, son."

It was the only welcome home he'd ever receive.

When Jack re-upped for his second tour of Viet Nam, Liz moved on. She was married now, to a stockbroker she'd met while working in New York. Her Dear John letter had come after her regular letters had begun to taper off. When he'd signed up for that second tour, she'd told him she couldn't wait any longer, and that she'd met someone else. Jack was neither surprised nor disappointed. He'd had a few encounters with the bar girls in Saigon, and a short fling in Hawaii with a surfer girl while on R&R between tours. Jack knew things were different now. He was not the innocent kid that had left Jersey City, and he'd never be the man she'd be expecting when he returned.

He would never talk to anyone about the things he'd seen and done in Viet Nam. His folded uniform would forever remain in a locked trunk. He stopped shaving, let his hair grow longer, regained some weight thanks to his mother's cooking, and pretended to be okay. He also pretended to look for a job. His mother encouraged him to go back to school, while his father just watched with sad eyes knowing all too well the post-combat fatigue his son was going through.

His boyhood friends who hadn't served seemed still to be children, and they'd all drifted away. Jack was uncomfortable in his own skin, and now a stranger in his hometown. He felt best when he was sitting on a ridge looking west over the Meadows beyond the city. He would watch the outbound freight trains bringing goods to the Western markets, and he'd feel a tugging at his core. He watched sunsets over the Meadows and heard the lonesome train whistles. Then one evening he just reached out and grabbed a westbound freight, as he'd often done as a kid. This one, however, didn't slow down enough for him to jump off until he was in Ohio. Then from Ohio, he stuck out a thumb.

Hitchhiking was easier in those days. Sometimes truckers on a long haul, sometimes an older couple looking for conversation. More often it was hippies in a beat-up van. The door would open, and a miasma of sweet-smelling smoke would roll out. Once a farmer in Kansas offered work, food, and lodging for help with the haying. Jack enjoyed the mindless work and would have stayed longer except the farmer, becoming aware of the glances between Jack and the farmer's wife, paid up his wages and sent him on his way. By the time he reached the front range of the Rockies, Jack was resigned, Viet Nam in his past. Also in his past was the ability or desire to ever live in a city again.

Changes in attitude from changes in altitude. Map therapy. He slowly migrated with the seasons to the Western slope of the Rockies. He did whatever work offered enough to keep him supplied and put gas in the old motorcycle he'd scored along the way. The bike was as much ownership as he wished to deal with.

His solitary life was softened by the occasional women he met along the way. They seemed to be a different species from the girls with whom he'd grown up. These girls wore bellbottom jeans, let their hair grow long and straight, and wore cowboy boots or hiking shoes. They told stories of hikes into the Grand Canyon and camping on the beaches of old Mexico. They came from small cities like Tucson or Santa Fe, or from farming communities in the Imperial Valley of California. They shared with him the same restlessness to see the country and not be tied down. They were free with their sleeping bags and knew how to start a one-match campfire. Then they, like he, would move on, leaving only a smile in their wakes.

It was one of the last Harvey Girls in the El Tovar Hotel in Grand Canyon Village that first lit Jack's fire for the American Southwest. He had finished a beer in the lodge bar and was sitting in the lobby thinking about what to do next when she walked into his life.

"I've seen you in here the last couple of days. Are you hiking in?"

Jack quickly stood, flustered by her beauty, and muttered, "No, I just wanted to look over the edge and see the Grand Canyon. Now that I've seen it, I was thinking of moving on."

She started to turn away, then stopped and studied him closely.

"Wake up, amigo! You can't see anything from the edge. I'm Carrie. I work here at the hotel. Or at least I did until this week. A different outfit bought the Harvey company, and things are about to change. I'm not staying, so I'm hiking down Hermit Trail tomorrow one last time. Want to come along?"

This chance encounter would change Jack's life.

Carrie slipped him into the girls' dorm that night where she, as a senior employee, had a single room. After letting their bodies slowly get to know each other, they fell into a soft sleep. Carrie woke him long before dawn, and she'd already provisioned for the hike.

Signing a logbook at the trailhead as the sun was just lighting the eastern horizon, they started off with Carrie in the lead. Jack was a little slow in seeing the vistas, since he was busy admiring the way her body moved carrying her pack. When he did look up from watching her stride, he stopped dead in his tracks. "I had no idea! You can't see any of this from the rim."

"I know, right? We're dropping two thousand feet in the first two miles. When I saw you in the lodge you looked like you needed this." She slightly readjusted her pack and walked on, with Jack following. They reached the river that evening, and the next two days were magic.

Carrie seemed to know everything about the canyon and delighted in telling him stories about Louis Boucher, known as the Hermit, of whom the trail was named, and about the wild burros that still inhabited the canyon, and she told him of the John Wesley Powell expedition, the first white men who had explored the canyon by river. Her voice was charged with reverence and sadness as she spoke of the first peoples who lived in the canyon and on the surrounding mesas. Her eyes grew moist as she spoke of how they'd been treated by the first settlers and soldiers.

The following nights were spent just listening to Hermit Rapid and its standing waves. Not speaking, just holding each other gently in the sleeping bags, absorbing the grandeur and watching the canyon walls change color in the fading twilight. On the third morning, Jack woke to seeing Carrie organizing her pack. "I need to head up, got stuff to do."

Jack looked away. "I'm not ready to leave yet."

"I know," she said. "You have some things to work out, and to let go of." She smiled and hugged him. "I left you all the food that I won't need on the hike up. Be sure you start out early enough, so you don't get caught in full sun on the Tonto Plateau on the way out." She kissed him once more and was gone before he could say anything more.

For the first time since Viet Nam, Jack felt completely at peace. As he explored the creek, he thought about how much he'd been affected by the women who'd recently come into his life. He had thought that travel and movement would give him direction. It was, however, the women who were connected to the West that stirred in him a sense of home he hadn't felt for a very long time, or even realized he'd been lacking. These women were fitted to their environment. They had a soft, sunlit beauty like evening alpenglow mixed with the vitality of the desert in bloom after a monsoon rain.

On the left side of Hermit Creek, where the stream meets the Colorado, there stands a cliff face with a wide ledge. From there one can look down on the river cutting through the canyon and see for a distance in both directions. Jack became aware of an approaching group of oar-powered dories and watched in admiration as they smoothly ran the rapid. He could faintly hear their shouts of encouragement and joy as they passed. Glancing further along the ledge, he saw a small rock cairn with a weathered stick poking out of it. Investigating closer, he saw a No. 10 can upside down in the cairn.

Under the can was an old-fashioned Mason jar with a note sealed inside. Typed on Desert Magazine letterhead was an account, dated July 21, 1947, of an expedition led by Norm Nevills in his boat the

Wren. This was Jack's date of birth, and the sense of synchronicity stunned him. Vowing to learn more of the people named on the expedition, Jack made a note before returning the artifact to its cairn. Kent Frost in Mexican Hat II. Otis "Doc" Marston in the Joan. Sandra was the third boat described in the story, which also mentioned the women on the trip. Maria Salifrank, Anna and Zoe Desloge, and Margaret Marston. Adventurous, Western women. In his mind Jack assigned the names of the historic Nevilles party to the boats he had just seen pass. He also knew that he'd seen his path, and that it would lead him home.

When Jack left the canyon the next morning, he rode his bike to Flagstaff and asked for a job at the raft company he had seen run the rapids.

Now, twelve years on, Jack had lost count of his trips down the "Big Ditch," as boatmen sometimes described the Grand Canyon. He'd become one of the company's senior river guides, and one day, while busily concentrating on rigging his boat at Lee's Ferry, he heard a familiar voice from the group of waiting clients.

"I guess the world really is round, and you've come a long way."

Looking up at Carrie, with her same beatific smile, he knew that this would be his best trip yet.

Otis Kunz is a retired ER nurse and a former ski instructor and boatman. He is a past member of a mountain rescue group, and a cancer survivor. He lives in Durango with his wife Helen and his daughter Sarah, herself a Grand Canyon boatwoman.

Wake Up to Your Wild Within

Shelli Rottschafer

What does it feel like to be alive?
Stand where
the force is greatest.
Only to hold the river
in your breath.

You could learn to live like this.
Pounding at you–
–time bound–
in your heart cavity.

Who turned on the light?
Knowing–
–you are alive–
as the planet bucks,
rears like a mustang
readied to throw you.

Time's stillness voices,
have you noticed yet?
until it quiets to murmur.
Pitters to silence–
–dies.

Poet, Educator, and Advocate Shelli Rottschafer (she/her/ella) completed her doctorate from the University of New Mexico in 2005 in Latin American Contemporary Literature. From 2006 until 2023 she taught at a small liberal arts college in Michigan as a Spanish Professor. Now she lives and writes in Colorado and New Mexico with her partner and their rescue pup.

The GOT Coop
Or,
How to Work Too Hard

M a d d y   B u t c h e r

L ike a lot of you, in the early months of the pandemic, I got chicks. Three little puff balls from the feed store, one black, one white, one reddish. For a time, they lived in a big cardboard box, with a heat lamp to keep them warm. They would need a coop, I realized, somewhat belatedly.

I got busy building one and challenged myself with making it entirely from scrap supplies I had kicking around the back side of the house.

This would be a *crème de la crème* coop. A fowl fortress.

I have some construction experience from years past. (After I got divorced, as a single mom with three young sons, I discovered I could make more money swinging a hammer than wielding a pen as a journalist. (How's that for the state of things?))

You could say I *probably, possibly* had enough experience to execute this utopian chicken villa plan.

First, I dug deep holes for four 4 x 4 posts and tamped them solidly into the ground. Then, with plywood and strapping, I built a floor and walls. I used a closet dowel rod for a roosting pole and built a shelf with dividers in case my laying hens didn't want to lay on the mezzanine. Why I had a sheet of plexiglass stashed at the backside of the house, I'm not sure. But with it, my darlings would have a lovely view of the yard.

I had one hinge. It was galvanized and nine inches across. I built a ten-inch door (big enough to use the hinge) and a ramp with raised wooden ridges for ease of stepping and entering. A sheet metal roof, with thoughtful overhangs for snow and shade, sealed the deal. The coop, like Winterfell in *Game of Thrones,* was ready to host the ladies and keep out all *personae non gratae.*

Come spring, with warmer days and nights, the princesses settled into their new environs.

Come fall, I decided to put my house on the market and move 40 miles west. Like a lot of you, I may not have fully appreciated the market's nuttiness. The place sold in a week. What followed was an absurdly fast-moving moving process, with dogs, horses, stuff, pandemic chickens and, of course, their colossal coop.

My friend Mark volunteered to help move it. I think this is something he regretted immediately. But Mark is a good friend.

Rather than dig up the 4 x 4 posts, I sawed them off at dirt level. We noted that it was still quite heavy and cumbersome. Imagine hefting a king-sized, 250-pound futon with sharp edges.

Given the consistently uneven, gravelly terrain, and its odd and awkward shape, no dolly could help. We muscled it into my horse trailer, with many cuss words and talk of *"ain't never doin' this again."*

Ah, but there was some *doin' this again.* Because of closing dates and home inspections and the finer details of moving oneself and one's trappings, Mark and I unloaded it at his house, for a five-day layover, then loaded it back into the trailer to what we assumed was its final destination, my new home.

For four years, the chickens enjoyed the coop. This year, we welcomed a few more chickens to the villa. A free-to-a-good-home duck joined them. All was well in the kingdom.

All was well until coyotes discovered and ate a hen who had inadvertently been closed out of the coop by a house sitter. We got on their dine-out route. Eventually, audaciously, the coyotes took to day-hunting my hens.

The decision was made to move them to the big city of Cortez. In the city, they would be safe with my son's hens. But, alas, the Cortez coop – one of those flimsy, prefabricated shacks – was too small for all the birds.

"You can have my coop!" I offered. Frugality or perhaps pity for the proud builder led him to say, "Okay."

On a Sunday afternoon, the coop caper began. Its movers were strong in number (three of us) but varyingly handicapped; I was nursing a recently broken wrist, my son had recently broken ribs and his shoulder, and his wife was pregnant.

With great, coordinated effort and screams to the high-spirited, oblivious toddler: "this will kill you if it falls on you!" we hefted it off the dirt, out of the fencing, and tipped it precariously into the truck bed, then strapped it down for the 20-mile ride to town. On its uneven 4 x 4 legs, it wobbled in the wind. We drove slowly, with the flashers on. I felt a little like Jed Clampett: "...*So they loaded up the truck and they moved to Beverly. Hills, that is. Swimming pools. Movie stars.*"

Only 50 feet to go!
In fading light, I backed to their six-foot-high backyard fencing.

We measured the width of the coop and the width of the gate. Hooray, it fits. Oh, but, no. We had neglected to take into account the metal roof and its thoughtful overhangs.

Given our handicaps and the coop's heft, simply hoisting it over the fence, like a laundry basket with fresh linens, was not an option. The kitchen table was brought to the yard and set in line with the truck bed. Inch by inch, we strenuously shuffled the coop through the gate and watched with relief as the roof cleared the top of the fence and rested temporarily on the table.

Only 40 feet to go!

It was dark. Without a place to call home, the hens paced back and forth, clucking with what I interpreted as angst. We donned headlamps and grunted the coop off the table, across the lawn, and into place. My daughter-in-law opened the door and welcomed the bewildered hens to their new, old abode.

High fives and beverages!

Under a moonless, rainy sky, I headed to the truck. "I'm going to miss that coop," I said to my son. "Maybe next summer, we could move it back."

Maddy Butcher is a free-lance journalist and producer of the Awe, Nice! *radio segment and podcast. She also day-works for Montezuma County ranchers.*

Orvis

A r t   G o o d t i m e s

Even on the Norwood
side of Dallas Divide
it's starting to be

that kind of San Juan cold
that rousts us from our snug aerie
looking south to Lone Cone

snow you can actually hear
rapping like a raven
against the glass

Siberian elms' low
groans between gusts
& the knee-deep cold.

Now's when
we bundle up. Put her into overdrive
& head down Norwood Hill

swerving for every
rock in the road
curving through the San Miguel Cañon

up Leopard Creek & down
to the Uncompahgre. Fifty miles
to the hot springs

just to see
steam billowing
Orion rising

and to once again
soak buck naked
in the Rockies' wild embrace

Poet, basketweaver, and former Green Party elected official in Colorado, Art Goodtimes served as Western Slope Poet Laureate (2011–2013), and is poetry editor for Fungi *magazine and the online anthology* Sage Green Journal *as well as director of the Telluride Institute's* Talking Gourds Poetry Program. *An earlier version of "Orvis" appeared in* Looking South to Lone Cone *(Western Eye Press, Sedona, AZ, 2013).*

Becoming a Man

Cynthia H. Chertos

All Dog Taxes Were Due July 1st, 1913.
All unlicensed dogs will be killed on sight
by the City Marshal after the date of this notice.
W.T. Black, Town Marshal
The Silverton Standard, July 12, 1913

June 10, 1913 – I turn 17 today. Mama kissed the top of my head whilst I was at the breakfast table. She cant hardly get to the top of my head if I stand up. She says I am nearly a man. I like the sound of that. Uncle Ralph came by after breakfast and said hes gonna make me into a real man one of these days. I dont think I like the sound of that.

June 14 – Sunny afternoon. Went down to the edge of the river with Mollie to fish. The rufus are back, chasin every other hummin-bird away from the wild flowers. Only thing is why do we have to have rufuses? Ther so mean. Chase the pretty ones away. Caught two trout. Mama is happy becaus were gonna have them for dinner. Kendall came down to play with Mollie. After fishin, cobbled together a miniature flyin machine with wood scraps Donny brought me from the mine. I still have to sand some of the pieces before its finished. My plan is to paint it and give it to Cousin Gilbert in a few days for his birthday. He will be 9.

June 16 – Mollie and me watched lots of birds out by the river today. We was real quiet. Mollie didnt bark once. I just laid on my back and watched them birds soar. And landin exactly on a dime wherever they want. If I could do anythin in the whole world, I would fly. I laid ther with my arms out and when I closed my eyes, I almost felt like I was flyin. When I went to stand up, I wanted to throw my crutch in the Animas. But then, not only could I not fly but I wouldnt be able to get around neither. Sometimes I hate that crutch.

June 17 – Cousin Benny thinks Im a sissy becaus I write in this book. I been keepin one since the 6th grade teacher made us do one over the summer and say all the stuff we did and what the weather was like and what happened around town and what we were thinkin about. And then to bring back when 7th grade began. I like doin it. Mama keeps a diary and no one calls her names. Uncle Ralph says if I have to write every day – like a girl, he said. A girl?? Anyways, he says I should call it a journal sos its more manly. Wonder if my pa wrote stuff down like I do.

Cousin Benny – I like him less and less as time goes. He is only 14 and hes already talkin about cuttin out on school and goin down the mines. I cant talk him out of it. Benny keeps tellin me Donny next door went down as a nipper when he was only 14. But I keep thinkin about Pa. What if Mr. Rattage had not had his candle fall and drop in the box of detonators? Maybe they would both be here still. Too many die down ther. I wouldnt go even if I could. I dont want Benny to go down ther neither. But he got his mind set.

I dont know why he wants to quit school. I miss school. Wish I could go back and do 10th grade over and over. Mrs. Brownlee, best teacher ever (and still calls me her rosy cheek young man), brought by another book. Its the newest Tom Swift. Tom and His Wizard Camera its called. Shes always bringin me books and I have liked every single one of them so I will this one too. Cousin Benny aint interested in readin. Little Cousin Gilbert does though.

June 19 – Folded laundry for Mama, as usual. Made a little airfield with wood scraps all lined out. Just the size for Cousin Gilberts flyin machine. Painted it red. Will take it over tomorrow. Sat in the field for a while and watched the birds again before supper. Lots of swallows. Flyin. Swoopin. Soarin. Wish I could tell one from another of its kind so I could name each one. Maybe not. Especially the ones Uncle Ralph might shoot down. Once I named our old chickens Ernestine and Madge. When they got too old to lay eggs, I couldnt eat them. Mama had to trade with Mrs. Deckman for some unnamed ones, sos we could have a nice Sunday dinner once in a while.

June 24 – Donny stopped out front on his way home from the mine and told me he heard a biplane was comin to Durango sometime soon. A guy said he saw a poster at the post office and Donny rushed over after work to see it. He knows I love them, all of them. Any kind. He does too. A curtis pusher, I think he said. 3 wheels underneath and that look feeble on the poster. Donny says it looks scary to fly. I would give anythin to go see it. I been cuttin articles about flyin machines ever since them Wright brothers when I was 8 years old. Got a stack under my bed. Hope Donny wasnt pullin my leg. But why would he? Folded more laundry for Mama.

June 25 – Mama went to town hall today to get Mollies license. I put it on her collar. A shiny brass oval with her number on it – 114 – and the year 1913. She says its hard enough feedin a dog, let alone payin a $5 tax just to have it around takin up space. She tried to make a joke. Said at least we dont have a circus becaus ther tax is $50 a day! A Kings Ransom she called it. She laughed but I know shes sore. But I know she would never get rid of Mollie. That dang dogs my best friend. Donny gave me a dime from his ma for fixin ther meat grinder. All it needed was a new bolt to hold the screw in. Old one was stripped. Think will give the dime to Mama toward the dog license.

June 28 – Last night I dreamed the right side of my body was as long as the left in every way. Both my legs were exactly the same length. And I was dancin with Carrie Lee. We had so much fun. Then I built myself a flyin machine and I flew all over Silverton and down the valley to Durango where I met up with the Wright Brothers. I could see all the earth from a birds eye view. I almost thought it was real til I woke up.

June 29 – Uncle Ralph tries hard to make up for me not havin a pa. As hes now a deputy to Marshal Black, he says he might be able to get me hired over ther. I wouldnt have to do much except sit at a desk and keep track of a bunch of papers. Mama is happy I might get a actual job. Ever since school got out last spring, shes worried I would never find work. Mines wont hire a cripple. Not many others neither. Not sure how I feel about Uncle Ralphs idea. Sure enough I do want to help support me and Mama. And wouldnt it be fine if Mama didnt have to take in laundry in addition to her work as a typewriter girl downtown. I think about it every time I see her rubbin clothes on that washboard, with that lye soap chappin her hands. If I cant help out, can I ever be a real man? But I dont think I want to work around Uncle Ralph. Not sure why. Just have a feelin.

June 30 – Mrs. Brownlee brought a huge stack of old newspapers today. Said the new school librarian was just goin to throw them away. And she thought I might like to have a look at them first. Most recent ones were on top. And sure enough ther bringin a Curtis biplane to Durango – in fall. I clipped it out. If I do get that job I will save every extra penny to be able to go.

July 1 – Whilst I was fixin letter E on Mamas typin machine, I could hear the younger boys callin out to get together a baseball game. I still have them feelins, like I wish I could play. I never tell Mama. I dont want her to think Im not happy as a lark. But heck. I still wish I could walk far enough just to watch them play way down by the wye. Stop all negative thought! Thats what Mama always says. After I unstuck the E, I went fishin. Caught 3 small ones. Mama is makin cornbread to go with. She will cook the guts for Mollie and when we are done I will throw her the fish skins too.

July 4 – The parade was fun. Reverend Johnson asked me to ride on the Congregational Church float. Carrie Lee was ther too. She asked me about how my summers goin and stuff like that. I could talk with Carrie Lee all day long. She likes to read books too. In the afternoon, I set up a stand and sold some of the toys I been makin with them wood scraps. Came home with 89¢. Would have been 90 but Carrie Lee only had 9 pennies. I would give it free, but her pa said she had to pay.

July 5 – Mama talked again today about me workin for Marshal Black. I heard her tell Uncle Ralph if he would do this one thing for his only sister she would be for ever greatful. She cant think of any-thin in the world would be a better opportunity for someone like me. I guess it might happen. Im lookin forward to bringin in some money besides a few ¢ from fixin things for neighbors or sellin my stupid homemade toys. The new sidewalk is goin in on the near side of the main street. Looks real fine. Carrie Lee was ther too. Watchin the diggin.

July 8 – Thursday. Rained all day. Mama couldnt do no laundry this morning so she slept in a little until 7. I made flapjacks for us both. Then I read more newspapers. Im almost thru the stack. Local ones and parts of ones from all kinds of places. Mostly big cities like New York and Chicago and Denver. Even one from London England that was printed before I was born. It was the most interestin of all with a big article on a guy name of Maxim who left America to live in England and invent a flyin machine with a whirlin arm above it. Wish I couldve seen that. I cut it out, but I wonder why would anyone leave America to live in England? Mama wants me to stow the newspapers in the shed so we got them for kindlin next fall when Im done cuttin.

July 13 – Uncle Ralph came over today. He said the Marshal was ready to hire me. We only had one thing to do first. I asked what and all he would say was he will pick me up before dawn tomorrow morning.

July 14 – Worst day of my life. Uncle Ralph drove me up and down streets in the dark. I asked what we were doin. He said we were huntin. I wasnt clear what you could hunt right in town. Then we came upon Kendall. Tommy and Buddys old hound. Uncle Ralph acts like this was excitin and Im not gettin his point. Kendall is a good old dog whos been around town forever. Sometimes comes down by the river when Mollie and me are fishin or just lookin up at the sky. Lays ther with us.

Uncle Ralph gets down and calls Kendall over and checks his neck. Then he pulls Kendall by his head right out to the middle of the road. He asks me, can I get down whilst he knows I cant get down on my own. So he puts a rope around Kendalls neck and ties the dog to the cart, then helps me down, real rough like so my spectacles go flyin and I have to use my crutch to pull them over. And whilst Im gettin my specs back on Uncle Ralph says I should show him Im a man. Then he shoves a pistol into my hand and says, shoot that dog son. That dog dont have a license on it. Its the law. Shoot it.

Im standin so close I almost could of scrubbed old Kendalls ears. I tell him I cant kill any dog, let alone one I know. He says a real man can shoot a dog. Especially a dog thats against the law. I felt scared and cold and my teeth chattered. Then Uncle Ralph says, real threatenin like. He says I cant have a job with the Marshal if I cant enforce the law as the Marshal sets it. I remember I turned my face away from Kendall. I seen the sun comin up. Uncle Ralph says if we dont do it now, ther will be people on the street soon and it will be too late. I prayed someone would come walkin down the street at that instant. He starts tellin me in no uncertain terms they only let me go to school all them years becaus I wasnt good for much else anyway. If I will not take this one chance to help support Mama, she would be better off if I was dead. Kill the dog. He says it over and over. And all I can hear in my head is Mama would be better off if I was dead. And I know how much that Marshals job means to her. Not just the money neither. But also her pride. Her boy workin to support the family. Her boy becomin a man. And Uncle Ralph grabs my arm and says stop cryin boy and you pull that trigger now or I will send you back home. Then he puts his hand over mine around the gun and puts his trigger finger on top of mine and presses that finger til it hurt. And then poor old Kendall lay ther dead. And Uncle

Ralph says well done boy. And I go over to the side of Cement St and puke my guts out. By then the sun was well up. Uncle Ralph threw Kendall in the back of the cart. And he took me to the Marshal for my first day of work.

Cynthia Chertos is a retired Congregational pastor from Silverton, where she continues living part-year. Her stories reveal the history and spirit of that former mining town, as well as its social and economic conditions over time. Her tales are described as "transporting imaginative historical fiction" (Kirkus Reviews).

Last Breath of the Colorado

Kenna Deen

The moss is green today—
not black
as desert skies weep for peace,
pleading with the man in the box
to unchain the Colorado.

Let her water run— wild, unbound,
a turquoise serpent chiseling stone,
her body no longer shackled by the calloused fists of men
who never had the right to hold her.

In 1983, she pummeled her cage
unheard,
unheeded,
and now she waits—
still as prayer,

swallowing sorrow,
as the dust drinks the last of her breath.

Yet still she hopes:
that pain carved deep by drought
will be enough to rouse her fury—
that thirst will birth a storm,
enough to let her scream.
That grief, long dammed,
will swell to wrath—
enough to make her rise,
roar,
flood the world awake:
at last—
Free.

Born in Gilbert, Arizona, Kenna Deen earned a degree in Environmental Engineering from ASU and moved to Durango shortly after. Ken has an adoration for nature and enjoys various outdoor activities, including rowing her boat down the river, climbing cracks in the desert, or foraging with friends in the forest.

War and Play Among the Hummingbirds

Katayoun Medhat

I fear I have brought war to the hummingbirds.

Ever since I installed the feeder, there has been incessant chasing, arguing, menacing, watch-keeping and fighting, none of which was, naturally, my intention to create.

What was my intention, you may ask?

Well, obviously it was to spend dreamy summer days on my little porch watching a community of dinky birds congregating, tiny bodies hovering over and perching on the swaying feeder, contentedly—and gratefully!—imbibing.

The operative word here is gratefully. We humans like to imagine ourselves the bountiful overlords of the natural realm, and all that we regale with our bounty as not much more than fur- and feather-clad stomachs.

Perhaps this is because our experience with the natural world is mostly limited to those parts of it which we have tamed, cunningly reducing wants and needs to what we can, or are willing to, provide.

Thus, what we imagine to be reflections of the natural world may be merely a depressed version thereof, creatures at our mercy confined to a gilded cage of a guaranteed meal a day, walkies at set times and treats for performing tricks, in exchange for forfeiting all other more complex, and more base, natural behavioral inclinations.

In his study of the gift, the anthropologist Marcel Mauss posited that gift-giving is not an altruistic act, but is always conditional and always bound to certain expectations.

My expectations, getting back to the hummingbirds, is to see them behaving as I want them to, that is with decorum, and with obvious appreciation of my largesse.

If there is appreciation, the hummingbirds do not express it in a way that is accessible to me. They twitter and tweeb indignantly, keep vigilant guard, ferociously dive-bomb any bird so brave as to attempt landing on the feeder, pursuing them furiously and at great distances.

The worst is the Rufus. Easily recognised by its bright copper marking, it patrols the feeder tirelessly, swooping on any bird even attempting to traverse the wider vicinity. Whenever the Rufus is here, things around the feeder are even more fraught than usual.

However, here an old German saying — *"When two are fighting, the third rejoices"* — proves quite true: there is one hummingbird (now my favorite), who watches and waits and judiciously calibrates furtive trips to the feeder to whenever its possible rivals are distracted by fighting. And when aren't they?

It is a wise bird, possibly an old bird, no longer interested in proving its superiority, no longer excited by these opportunities of assertion through petty skirmishes, by which its tribe is apparently compelled to show its physical prowess.

But — wait! Maybe this is it? Maybe all this fighting isn't about the feeder at all, but is rather about the opportunity to practice fighting, just as the Olympic Games were, originally, an opportunity to test fitness for warfare: *"This time take the medal. Next time it will be death."*

Perhaps my feeder's significance to the hummingbirds is not so much as a dispenser of sugar water (one part pure white cane sugar to four parts water, if you fancy creating your own personal battle-field), but an entertaining opportunity in halcyon days to train for times of starvation and disaster.

What about the "feast and famine" thing, then? Is it a thing?

Maybe hummingbirds know that the shadow of famine looms over the feast, always. Just as we humans, on some level, know that we always walk, if not *in*, then toward the valley of death.

I have known children, in particular boys, who would spend all of their free time playing war games of one type or another. At one time I reacted to boys playing war games just as I do now to hum-mingbirds fighting over the feeder: I found playing at war unspeak-ably obscene, a waste of time and creativity, a gratuitous evocation of destruction.

But looking at the hummingbirds, it now occurs to me that may-be these games aren't about playing at war.

Maybe playing war games is about coming to terms with the existence of war; the acceptance, via play, of something that is the very opposite of play—which I would, at one time (before I started writing this piece), have defined as the life-affirming, joyful, spon-taneous, exuberant and extravagant expenditure of surplus energy.

Not any more.

Play may be joyful, spontaneous, exuberant and all that, but it takes place in the valley of the shadow of starvation, war and death, and is always, always a preparation for darker times to come.

Never trust a feeder.

The hummingbirds have taught me that.

Katayoun Medhat spends her summers in the Four Corners, watching hummingbirds, and her winters in the south of England, delighting in the well-mannered feeder behavior of blue tits (thereby disproving the central hypothesis of this essay). She is the author of the Milagro Mysteries. Find her on: www.katayounmedhat.com

· POEM ·

Where I'm Headin'

Maddy Butcher

I don't cotton to no church with walls or bylaws,
but I get down on my knees for Nature.

Take them horses,
Why, they deliver homilies every day.
Straight shooters.
Nothing thorny.

It's just a matter of knowing their vernacular
and showing up,
Not just Sundays, but every day.

And, heck, my ass always feels better in a saddle
than a pew.

Maddy Butcher is a free-lance journalist and producer of the Awe,
Nice! *radio segment and podcast. She also day works for Montezuma
County ranchers.*

Extra, Extra, Read All About It

Gail Binkly

Anne Hunter looked up from her notes and into the eyes of a tall, smiling, boyish-faced man standing silent as a lamppost in front of her desk.

How long had he been there? It was impossible to tell. Once again she silently cursed the receptionist, who, as was her wont, had allowed a visitor to wander unannounced into the newsroom.

"May I help you?" she asked the young man, mustering all her patience. He was thin and gawky; his eyelashes fluttered nervously as she spoke. His eager face irritated her. He looked like a student at the local community college, all unsquelched hopes and dreams.

"Can you print this?" he asked, handing her a folded sheet of paper from a yellow legal pad.

Unfolding it, she deciphered the penciled attempt at a press release:

POPULAR PROFESSOR FORCED TO LEAVE!

Known for his innovative and effective teaching style, his extensive work with the community as an instructor of electronics engineering courses, and his deep involvement in significant research at Crystal Community College, the highly-regarded Calvin Edwards has been terminated after two years. During which time he re-vamped the entire electronics engineering program. He also raised by over 50% the number of students in the basic electronics class.

"I was told that the reason for my abrupt termination was that there were budget cuts," said Professor Edwards. "I am truly saddened to hear this and feel that the school should re-examine its priorities."

The college and especially his electronics engineering students will feel a great loss at the departure of Professor Edwards. Many believe the electronics engineering program will never be the same.

Well, there might be a story in it, Anne decided, since she was not the education reporter and would not have to deal with the sad case of Professor Edwards. Who, of course, was not truly a *professor*, merely an instructor, if the "press release" was right.

"May I have your name and number?" she asked.

"Why?"

"I'll give this to the education reporter and she may want to contact you if she has any more questions. She may want some quotes from you or other students about Mr. Edwards."

He hesitated a moment, then said, "I *am* Professor Edwards."

"Oh!" Anne stared fixedly at the sheet of paper, not daring to meet the man's eyes lest she burst into laughter. "Well, um, thank you. Write your number on the bottom."

She swiveled in her chair and pretended to be busily studying something in a stack of newspapers on a table behind her. After a long silence she judged that he must have left, and dared a glance around her. She was alone. The other desks in the small newsroom sat empty.

None of the desks matched; one was of metal, two were of pressed wood with different fake-wood finishes, and one was of battered mahogany and missing a drawer. Their chairs likewise were all unique, with individual quirks and weaknesses. Anne's, for instance, was a comfortable swivel chair with a springy seat, but if you leaned back in it more than a few degrees, it would suddenly tip over, pitching its occupant onto the floor.

In the far corner of the room, behind a strangely incongruous Chinese screen, the desk of the advertising director, Marjean, was likewise empty.

Anne rose, laid the sheet of yellow paper on Nicole's desk without attaching a note—let her wonder where it had come from—and sat back down at her own typewriter.

Late-afternoon heat lay like a pall over the windowless room. The police scanner flickered silently in the corner; not a thing was happening, not even a minor traffic accident. It was two o'clock on Friday, and all across Colorado, women like her were doubtless gearing up for a busy weekend, preparing to rush home and primp for excursions to fancy parties or elegant restaurants.

Here in Crystal Waters, a tiny berg named for a spring on the Western Slope, there was no such hope of excitement. The entertainment options were few: Go to the town's only movie theater, which was showing some bloody "monster stalks girl" flick; slip inside one of the town's numerous bars, which at least had working swamp coolers, and be ogled by the young ranchers hoping for a little Friday-night action; or enjoy a moderately good meal at one of several local restaurants, whose menus Anne knew by heart. ("The Mayor Spencer Burger. A robust quarter-pound of meat grilled just the way you like it, smothered in American cheese, served with a heaping plate of our famous fries.")

Anne decided she would just go home, have a small, healthful meal, then relax in the tub and read.

With a sigh she returned to finishing her story about Tuesday's meeting of the Crystal Waters City Council, which had voted unanimously not to restrict semis from idling, parking, or doing whatever their owners pleased within city limits. A timid ordinance that would have restricted them to 30 minutes of idling and not allowed them to park in residential areas for longer than one week had been shot down after an armada of burly truck-drivers packed the council chambers, loudly complaining that their rights were being curtailed and that Crystal Waters was coming to resemble Communist Russia. Even the ordinance's originator had voted against it in the end.

"Drivin' a truck is the American way! What are you a-tryin' to do, turn us into a bunch of pinkos?"

Anne jumped in her seat. Michael's voice had so echoed her own thoughts that it took her a moment to realize he had come into the room. It was a half-hour from deadline, but he was just now slouching into his chair ten feet from hers after taking a glance at what she was writing.

"Where have you been?" she asked. Michael habitually stretched deadlines, but he wasn't usually THIS late.

"A ribbon-cutting for the new JCPenney's outlet, did you forget? It's going to save downtown Crystal! How's the truck story coming?"

"I have a lot of lively quotes," she grinned.

"No doubt. Well, I guess I'd better get started. Where's Howard?"

"Downstairs."

Michael cocked an eyebrow upward. "Weather report?"

"Fair to partly cloudy." Howard, the editor-in-chief, had had only a couple of drinks at lunch and was in a relatively mellow mood. Right now he was below with the production people, batting out headlines for the inside pages and watching the paste-up process. Anne was glad – it was far easier to write when he wasn't around, breathing nervously and eyeing the clock.

"Well, it was definitely stormy earlier," Michael said. "Something was wrong with his typewriter — how you can get keys to stick on an IBM Selectric, I don't know, but something was wrong — and he was calling it a 'damn lousy stinking machine' when Marjean walked by and thought he said, 'damn lousy stinking Marjean,' so you can imagine the problems that caused."

Howard and Marjean coexisted in a state of mutual antagonism.

Anne chuckled, but stopped abruptly when she saw a woman walking into the newsroom and marching up to her desk. She had plump pink cheeks, soft lips and round blue eyes under wavy silver hair. But there was nothing soft about her voice, which grated like a badly played violin.

"Don't you have any checks and balances here?" she demanded,

Anne remembered who she was – Mrs. Leon Garlow, a resident of nearby Quail Creek. She had brought in a handwritten obituary last week for her father-in-law. Anne herself had typed it up.

"How can I help you?" Anne asked.

"You put the wrong number in the obituary!"

"What wrong number?"

"The number of the American Legion Post! It was supposed to be 37 and you put 39!"

Anne recalled struggling to read the tangled handwriting in the obit. She was ashamed to realize she did not actually know the number of the local American Legion Post and had not thought to check it.

"I'm so sorry," she said. "We'll reprint the obituary with the correct American Legion Post number in our next issue."

"Well, why did you put the wrong one in there in the first place?"

"I had a little trouble reading it – "

Mrs. Garlow cut her off. "Don't make excuses."

"Ma'am, as I said, we will reprint the obituary. That should take care of the problem."

"Take care of it? Everyone in town has seen it. It said my father-in-law was with Post 39. There is no Post 39 here. Everyone is talking about it."

"I'm sure Quail Creek is in an uproar," Michael mumbled dryly from his corner.

Mrs. Garlow glanced at him sharply. "What did you say?"

"I just don't understand what you want, other than for us to reprint the obituary," Anne said, clinging to the last vestiges of her patience.

"What do I want? What do I want, missy? I want this newspaper to run an apology on the front page. An apology to me, my husband, his father, may he rest in peace, and our whole family."

"Well, I don't have the authority to do that," Anne said, adding with malicious pleasure, "you'll have to talk to our editor, Howard Trent."

"And where is he?"

"He's very busy right now," Michael interjected. "We're on deadline for tomorrow's paper. I'm sure if you come back Monday –"

"You'd better believe I will, and I'll be reporting your insolence, both of you." Mrs. Garlow spun her well-padded body around with surprising speed and made an angry exit.

Michael laughed, and Anne turned hastily back to her story. The clatter of their typewriters made the newsroom seem suddenly lively. That sound, and the rumble of the printing presses, always made her think of Woodward and Bernstein and the *Washington Post*. She'd started work as a journalist just before they brought down President Nixon, but they inspired her even now, several years later. Maybe someday *she* would write something that really mattered.

She finished her article at three, the ostensible deadline, but Howard had not appeared from below. Michael, meanwhile, was banging away rapidly. Whatever else you thought about him, you had to admit he was fast. By three-thirty he had batted out twenty inches about the new Penney's outlet.

"Here," he said, ripping the pages from the typewriter and thrusting them at her. "Where's yours?" They edited each other's stories, as Howard's idea of editing was to run a glance diagonally down each page and murmur, "Good, good."

Anne got a pencil ready, but she knew she would have little reason to use it. Michael *was* good. Why he worked at this backwater was beyond her comprehension, unless it was because of his complete lack of respect for authority. Even in the supposedly free-wheeling, iconoclastic newspaper business, editors and publishers liked people who would kiss up to them.

She looked at Michael's lead.

"With a skillful slash of his scissors, Mayor Greg Spencer cut a pink ribbon and cleared the way Friday for the hordes of shoppers expected to patronize the new JCPenney's outlet in downtown Crystal Waters."

Anne smiled. He put his heart into even the most banal topics.

"What have you got?" came Howard's voice at last as he emerged from the stairwell, a thin yet somehow doughy man who looked perpetually tired. He never had a list of stories or planned them in advance; he expected the reporters to come up with *something* for each of the two issues published per week, but he didn't much care *what* they came up with.

"The Penney's opening," Michael said. "Twenty inches. The pictures are already downstairs."

"I've got, um, forty inches on the big fight at City Hall over trucks in town," Anne said. "There were probably seventy-five people there. The place was packed. The police chief even came to keep the peace."

"Sounds good, sounds good. And we've got, what, a feature on paint horses from Nicole? Let's see, we'll lead with the Penney's, and then the truckers."

Michael rolled his eyes at Anne. Anything that was judged to be "positive" news, especially regarding potential advertisers such as Penney's, took precedence over genuine news such as the truck ordinance's failure. She shrugged. In a paper as small as this one, most everything got read no matter where it was placed.

Howard grabbed the sheets of paper from their hands and scanned them. "Nice, nice," he murmured. "Okay, Anne, you can go. Michael, you want to help with headlines?"

"Sure," he said, following Howard down the stairs to the basement, which housed the light tables and presses.

Once again, she was alone in the newsroom. Howard had said she could go, but she thought she'd get a little start on a feature she was doing about a student at the local high school who had made it to the state track meet in the high jump.

"They said it couldn't be done," she typed. "They said a kid who was just five-foot-six couldn't . . ."

Her concentration was shattered when the police scanner, which until now had been silent except for a few bursts of idle chitchat from bored officers, began emitting three different, shrill signals.

Anne frowned; it sounded like they were calling the sheriff . . . and an ambulance . . . and someone else. Was it a car crash? It didn't quite sound like it, but automatically she pulled her camera out of her bottom drawer. Accident photos were a mainstay of the front page.

"Ten-thirty-five," the dispatcher said. "Ten-thirty-five. Please respond to fourteen three twenty-five County Road T. We have one gunshot victim, possible frank. Repeat. Fourteen three twenty-five County Road T. Shooting victim, possible frank."

A ten-thirty-five was dispatch code for a major crime; Anne hadn't heard that number since she left her previous job in Colorado Springs. "Frank" meant fatality, though why dispatchers couldn't just say "fatality," she didn't know.

She grabbed the telephone and dialed the sheriff's office. The phone rang a long time but finally a woman answered.

"This is Anne Hunter with the *Crystal Courier*. Has there been a homicide?"

A long silence followed. The woman, who had not identified herself, said at last, "Yes. We'll have a press release brought over to you in one hour."

"Can you tell me any more right now?" Anne tried to ask, but the woman had hung up.

Anne charged down the stairs and found Howard and Michael bent over a light table, looking at the front page, which was not entirely finished. Two of the paste-up women were walking back and forth carrying strips of waxed paper and sticking them onto different pages.

"There's been a murder," Anne said. "We need to hold the paper."

Howard looked up with a grim, tired expression. "We can't afford to pay a bunch of overtime. It'll make a good story for Wednesday's paper."

"But the sheriff's office said they'd send us a press release in an hour. We can surely wait that long! Wednesday – that's forever for something this big."

Michael turned to Howard. "We can leave a little space for a story at the top of the page and finish everything else. Anne can write to space."

Howard shook his head. Clearly, he was ready to go home. "Maybe we can do an extra this weekend."

Anne stared at him blankly. An extra? That sounded like something from the 1950s. And how would that save them any money in overtime?

"C'mon," Michael coaxed Howard. "Let's wait one hour and

Anne can write up whatever is in the release."

Howard drew in an enormous breath and exhaled it slowly. "All right," he said. "But if that release doesn't come in an hour, forget it."

For the next hour, Michael had the paste-up women rearrange the front page, leaving room for a twelve-inch story across all six columns at the top. Anne hovered near the front door. She wanted to rush to the sheriff's office, but she knew they did not like her showing up there.

It was an hour and two minutes after her phone call when a deputy pulled up in front of the newspaper office and strode to the front door.

"Here," he said, handing Anne a sheet of paper.

"Thank you," she said, smiling, but he left without smiling in return.

She ran inside and found Michael waiting for her. She held the release out so they could both read it. It said:

PRESS RELEASE

FOR IMMEDIATE RELEASE

OFFICE OF SHERIFF ERIC BEADLE

On Friday afternoon at 4:11 p.m., sheriff's officers were called to the home of John R. Pryor, 14325 County Road T. They found the deceased body of a woman.

The sheriff's office is investigating.

Michael looked at her. "You're going to have a little trouble getting twelve inches out of that," he said dryly.

In the end, Anne managed to bleed six inches out of the release. She led with a statement that there was a probable homicide, then typed in the entire release, and finally stated at length that she could get no official comment from the sheriff's office.

The headline, which was sixty-four points in size, read, "Murder

Near Crystal Waters."

Headlines without verbs were a specialty of Howard's.

But the story was not at the top of the page. Howard had decided it was too short to be the main article.

Above her article was a different story, also with a six-column headline. It was seventy-two points, meaning it was an inch high – about the size of "Japanese Bomb Pearl Harbor" or something similarly world-shattering.

It read, "JCPenney's Store to Bring Dollars."

Gail Binkly is a journalist who also writes fiction. Her first novel, Trek of a Bird-Woman, *is an adventure fantasy tale. She lives in Cortez.*

· POEM ·

The Dove Creek Farm in Dreams

Ellen Hill Robinson

The bones of the colt,
the bones of the calf,
dried carcasses caught on barbed wire –
the kittens are frozen;
the rabbit is, too -
The carnivorous cat
shall expire.

Those barbed wire fences
they cling
and they scrape
and the rusty nails, they do, too;
and they pierce, when they can,
according to plan,
the worn-out sole of your shoe.

The snakes and
the spiders,
the black widow liars,
the coils, the rattles
the hoes - Call Daddy, he'll come
don't scream and don't run.
He'll chop off their heads, just like so.

The dried old barn
ever empty and cold
the vacant hayloft aghast
the smells
the trails
the coffee-tin pails
the spells we so carelessly cast –

And the nightmares they come
and the nightmares they stay
and the nightmares flow on until dawn.
Rattlesnakes slither around my neck,
and the baby ghost's blood tiptoes on.

Abandon the shack.
Abandon the shed.
The cellar is empty and cold.
We are who we are –
we wait from afar
until the dear old farm is sold.

And the nightmares they come
and the nightmares they play
and the nightmares dance on until dawn.

Rattlesnakes slither around my neck,
and baby ghost's blood scurries on.

Ellen Hill Robinson is a teacher and writer, born and raised in the Four Corners Area, who now divides her time between the Denver area and Dolores. Her great grandparents homesteaded near Cortez in the early 1900's, and her kin have lived and breathed the Four Corners' enchantment ever since.

Four Corners, Four Mountains, One Homeland

Stephen Trimble

The bullseye of "Four Corners" falls within the Colorado Plateau, the vast redrock heart-shape at the center of the West. This decisive crisscross—the arbitrary result of following lines of longitude and latitude, meridians and parallels, to define place—also happens to be the fulcrum of my experience, the epicenter of my home landscape.

I've lived in the Four Corners states all my life.

National and territorial history created this cartographic anomaly 160 years ago, the only spot in the nation where four states meet. And the jurisdictions meeting at Four Corners aren't just four states but two sovereign Native nations, as well—the Ute Mountain Ute Reservation in Colorado and the Navajo Nation in the other three quadrants.

I stand at the Four Corners monument, and I can sense the landscapes of each state sweeping away from me. I turn to the north and picture the looming Rockies beyond the canyons and mesas of Colorado and Utah. I circle to the east, and I know that halfway across New Mexico the Rio Grande slices the state in half, the great river flowing toward Mexico and into the Chihuahuan Desert. I keep rotating, toward the Arizona deserts to the south, and then to the west, where I travel in my mind's eye through Utah to the Great Basin.

Four Corners is a perch, an intersection. From this still point, sight lines lead outward—but also inward. Imagine all these reeling-away landscapes reversing direction and convening and concentrating their energies here in this one spot. All the spiritual energy of the wildlands and human inhabitance/inheritance of the West pouring into a single point on the map. In this way, the Four Corners resembles a Pueblo place of emergence, a *sipapu*, and a point of convergence, too—an energy vortex like those revered by New Agers on pilgrimages to Sedona or Mount Shasta.

From here, I feel the breadth of my home landscape.

Like many Westerners, I have moved from place to place, and my sense of home has grown to include a major expanse of the West. But I need reference points, boundaries. And so I have embraced the Indigenous concept of mountains bounding sacred home ground. It's presumptuous and perhaps inappropriate for a non-Native, but to me it is humbling and nourishing to make this bow of respect toward my own homeland. It's one way to comprehend just where I live on the surface of the earth.

As a writer, I spent a decade in my thirties and forties listening to Southwest Native people, interviewing everyone from high school students to elders. Over and over, I heard them speak of land as sacred and mountains as holy places.

Navajo people, the Diné, traditionally define their home within the boundaries of four sacred mountains, one at each of the four cardinal directions. Within this rough circle of land lies everything good, everything needed to live well. Many Native people speak of the mountains overlooking their homes with reverence, affection, and awe.

I admire this gesture of paying attention to the land. For mountain peaks give us a focus in a land where the sky and prairie, plateau and desert are daunting in scale. Mountains break up the awesome Western space; they form the walls of the rooms—the lowlands—where people live and highways and railways pass through.

Most anywhere in the West, we do not live *in* the mountains, we live at their feet—in cities, towns, and ranches built in dry places dependent on mountain watersheds. Without water, people move on.

From these outposts we look across long horizons to where the moon and sun break over the rim of the earth, past silhouettes of nearby peaks. The proverbial "comforts of home" begin to include the landscape surrounding our warm houses—a panorama distinguished by landmark peaks.

We learn the names of the mountains. And as we acknowledge the long tenancy of Native people, we learn, too, of each tribe's anchoring landmarks. Western Apache people told anthropologist Keith Basso that "wisdom sits in places." Without aspiring to wisdom, I believe our lives grow richer when we pay attention to place, when we link our lives to landscape and allow mountains to help define our home.

I grew up in Denver, keeping an eye out for the horizon line of the Front Range, smoke-blue in summer, ice-white in winter. Longs Peak, with its blocky summit, was the highpoint of Rocky Mountain National Park and the northernmost "fourteener" I could see. My father loved to join me in watching for its distinctive silhouette; we picnicked at alpine lakes below the peak. Later, in college I attempted a winter ascent with my buddies and, still later, even wrote a book about the mountain. But mostly Longs Peak feels like family—a cherished backdrop that's been with me since childhood.

After college, I lived in Tucson for a time, watching the moon set in a pastel pre-dawn sky beyond Baboquivari Peak, the great blunt stub off to the southwest, central to the creation narrative of the Tohono O'odham people who looked up to its summit each day. Baboquivari—wild chiles growing in its canyons, caracaras wheeling over its saguaros—stood for me as a marker, a symbol of the power and soothing warmth of the desert.

From Tucson, I moved to northern Arizona, to Flagstaff, and lived in the protective shadow of the San Francisco Peaks. A Navajo man, Steve Darden, spoke to me about these peaks, sacred to his people:

"That mountain has life. That mountain has a spirit. That mountain has a holiness.

"The Holy People live there. Because of that, it's a place where I can find refuge, rebirth. I garner strength from this mountain—spiritually, from this place."

I think of the Peaks from a distance, watching clouds build in summer monsoon season over the elegant angles of their dignified summits. I see the Hopi villages perched on mesas jutting like ship's prows over the arid plateau country that climbs from bare sandstone and twisting junipers to the one snow-covered landmark in sight, the graceful curve of the San Francisco Peaks.

These 12,000-foot summits stand as beacon and promise. They reassure us with their life and lush fertility in a region known more for naked canyons and unnerving glimpses into geologic time.

They are the most hallowed mountains in the Southwest. Everything falls away from their summits. They stand at the center of the universe.

With a move to New Mexico in the 1980s, I lived in a Pueblo landscape. My house in the Rio Grande Valley lay on the axis between Tsikomo at the summit of the Jemez Mountains, and Truchas Peak along the crest of the Sangre de Cristo Range. Pueblo people still make pilgrimages to shrines atop these peaks, leaving offerings of cornmeal, prayer feathers, bits of bone and broken pottery.

I liked walking outside in the mornings to look up to the mountains and say their names: *"Tsikomo. Truchas. Tsikomo."*

Truchas, with a gaping cirque on its face, rises to 13,102 feet, the second highest mountain in New Mexico. Tsikomo, a rounded dome on the rim of the Jemez caldera, has a distinctive meadow just below its peak, the only treeless patch on the western horizon.

"Tsikomo."

Now, in Salt Lake City, I live beneath the Wasatch Front. Just over the shoulder of the first rise of peaks stands Mount Timpanogos, the dominant mountain of the Wasatch Range. Massive and commanding, Timpanogos stands on Ute and Shoshone land. I can feel it out there now.

Longs Peak, Truchas, Baboquivari, Timpanogos. I've chosen these mountains. Between them stretches my home. In the center place of this land stand the San Francisco Peaks, consecrated to all who dwell nearby.

As I traverse this territory, I note the mountain ranges, anticipating the next landmark coming up from beneath the horizon. The roll of the hills takes me through the litany of life zones, up from desert grassland through piñon-juniper woodland and into fragrant ponderosa pines standing still and friendly in the sun. Or down through the concentric circles of desert shrubs—sagebrush, saltbush, greasewood, creosote—toward the austere playas that form the power spots, the chakras, of Basin and Range country.

Indigenous people root their spirituality in landscape. Laguna Pueblo scholar Paula Gunn Allen says, simply, "We are the land." Over and over, Southwest Native people have told me that the crux of their lives is simple: acknowledgment is the key, paying attention to the Earth and giving thanks for its blessings. To live with reciprocity, to listen to the Earth, we need only relax and open our senses.

Those of us not steeped in these relationships need to work a bit to tap into this healing power of the earth. To sense the land, to feel the earth stretching away from you, rising to the mountains, means paying attention. It happens incrementally, step by step. Four Corners, Four States, Four Mountains, One Homeland.

I write this in the house where I live, in the domain of Mount Timpanogos. I make pilgrimages, to walk the wildflower meadows of my designated mountain of the north, to stomp through the first snow reaching down into the foothills to blanket the leafless oaks and maples.

I look out from Timpanogos to the four directions, to the four corners of the West, and dream out to the limits of my home.

Colorado native and (now) Utah writer and photographer Stephen Trimble has won significant awards for his nonfiction, his fiction, and his photography. His 25 books on Western wildlands and Native peoples include The People: Indians of the American Southwest *and* Bargaining for Eden. *See www.stephentrimble.net for more of his work.*

About the Editors

Gail Binkly (Essays) is a career writer, reporter, and editor. In 2023, she published her first novel, *Trek of a Bird-Woman*, an epic fantasy adventure. She has a master's degree in journalism from the Ohio State University and taught news-editorial writing for nine years at the University of Southern Colorado, now Colorado State University-Pueblo. She worked as a sportswriter at the Colorado Springs *Gazette* and as a reporter and managing editor at the *Cortez Sentinel*, now the Cortez *Journal*. For twenty years she published and edited a monthly newspaper, the *Four Corners Free Press*, in Cortez, Colorado. The Colorado Society of Professional Journalists honored her with its Keeper of the Flame lifetime achievement award in 2024. She lives with her husband and cats in Cortez, where she continues writing and reporting.

Sarah Carr (Poetry) grew up in the Sierra, and found home in the Pacific Northwest and Appalachia before mountains and deserts drew and rooted her in Colorado in 2010. She holds a BA in creative writing and an MA in literature, and has worked in education for seventeen years as a college writing instructor, university curriculum coordinator, secondary English teacher, and outdoor educator. Her writing has appeared in an eclectic range of publications, from *The Climbing Zine* to *The Journal of the Wooden O* to the inaugural 2024 edition of the *Four Corners Voices* anthology. She writes poetry, lives in an old barn in Mancos with her dog Modus and piles of bikes and books, and teaches composition, literature, and outdoor skills. She is honored to curate and amplify the chorus of talented local poets in this year's anthology.

Chuck Greaves (Stories), the author of seven novels, has been a finalist for many of the top honors in crime fiction including the Shamus, Lefty, Macavity, and Audie Awards, as well as the New Mexico-Arizona, Oklahoma, and Colorado Book Awards and the Harper Lee Prize for Legal Fiction. His novel *Tom & Lucky* (Bloomsbury) was a *Wall Street Journal* "Ten Best Mysteries of 2015" selection, while his novel *The Chimera Club*, the fourth installment in his critically acclaimed Jack MacTaggart series of legal mysteries (Minotaur), was a 2023 Colorado Book Award finalist and was named the Best Mystery Novel of 2022 by the Colorado Authors' League. When not writing, he farms wine grapes in McElmo Canyon, and you can visit him at: www.chuckgreaves.com.

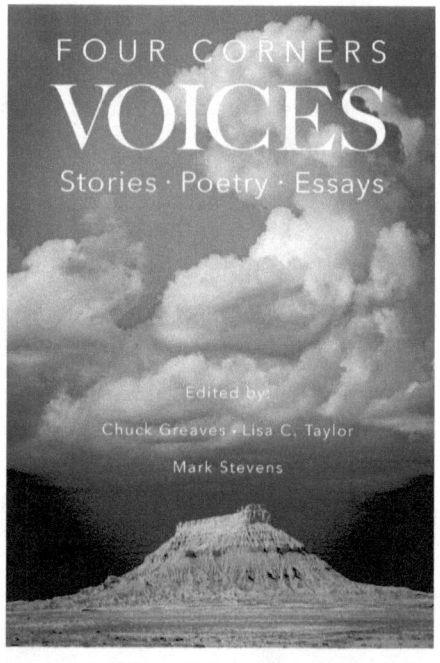

www.ingramcontent.com/pod-product-compliance
Lightning Source LLC
Chambersburg PA
CBHW021423110726
47901CB00008B/2272